Praise for the Plays of Neil LaBute

REASONS TO BE PRETTY

"What makes this play resonate is less its Big Theme—beauty (or lack thereof) and its discontents—than how that theme illuminates the insecurities of people who don't feel they have much to offer the world." **—BEN BRANTLEY,** *The New York Times*

"LaBute's most adult story—or at least, his most touching tale—primarily because its struggling hero, if you can call him that, really does want to grow up."

—MICHAEL KUCHWARA, *San Francisco Chronicle*

"The play raises provocative ideas about beauty—the significance it holds and the anxieties it creates. Even more fascinating is the underlying theme LaBute has explored ever since his breakthrough work, *In the Company of Men*—when men get together, the result is toxic."

—JOE DZIEMIANOWICZ, *New York Daily News*

IN A DARK DARK HOUSE

"Refreshingly reminds us . . . that [LaBute's] talents go beyond glibly vicious storytelling and extend into thoughtful analyses of a world rotten with original sin." **—BEN BRANTLEY,** *The New York Times*

WRECKS AND OTHER PLAYS

THIS IS HOW IT GOES

"LaBute's . . . most sophisticatedly structured and emotionally complex story yet, this taut firecracker of a play about an interracial love triangle may do for liberal racism what David Mamet's *Oleanna* did for sexual harassment."

—JASON ZINOMAN, *Time Out New York*

"This prolific playwright . . . has topped even his own scary self in this unrelentingly perilous, disgracefully likeable 90-minute marvel about race, romance and our inability to know everything about just about anything . . . The only unambiguous thing about this astonishing play is its quality." —LINDA WINER, *Newsday*

"The most frank, fearless look into race relations from a white dramatist since Rebecca Gilman's *Spinning into Butter.*"

—ELYSA GARDNER, *USA Today*

FAT PIG

"The most legitimately provocative and polarizing playwright at work today." —DAVID AMSDEN, *New York*

"The most emotionally engaging and unsettling of Mr. LaBute's plays since *Bash* . . . A serious step forward for a playwright who has always been most comfortable with judgmental distance." —BEN BRANTLEY, *The New York Times*

"One of Neil LaBute's subtler efforts. [It] demonstrates warmth and compassion for its characters missing in many of LaBute's previous works [and] balances black humor and social commentary in a . . . beautifully written, hilarious dissection of how societal pressures affect relationships [that] is astute and up-to-the-minute relevant." —FRANK SCHECK, *New York Post*

THE SHAPE OF THINGS

"LaBute is the first dramatist since David Mamet and Sam Shepard—since Edward Albee, actually—to mix sympathy and savagery, pathos and power . . . *The Shape of Things* . . . continues his obsession with the power games men and women play."
—DONALD LYONS, *New York Post*

"LaBute . . . continues to probe the fascinating dark side of individualism . . . [His] great gift is to live in and to chronicle that murky area of not-knowing, which mankind spends much of its waking life denying."
—JOHN LAHR, *The New Yorker*

"*Shape* . . . is LaBute's thesis on extreme feminine wiles, as well as a disquisition on how far an artist . . . can go in the name of art . . . Like a chiropractor for the soul, LaBute is looking for realignment, listening for the crack."
—JOHN ISTEL, *Elle*

Neil LaBute
filthy talk for troubled times and other plays

NEIL LABUTE is a critically acclaimed playwright, filmmaker, and fiction writer. His controversial works include the plays *bash: latterday plays, The Distance from Here, The Mercy Seat, Fat Pig* (winner of the Outer Critics Circle Award for Outstanding Off-Broadway Play, Olivier nominee for Best Comedy), *Autobahn, This Is How It Goes, Some Girl(s), Wrecks and Other Plays, In a Dark Dark House*, and *Reasons to Be Pretty* (Tony nominee for Best Play); the films *In the Company of Men, Your Friends and Neighbors, Nurse Betty, Possession, The Wicker Man, Lakeview Terrace,* and *Death at a Funeral*; the play and film adaptation of *The Shape of Things*; and the short-story collection *Seconds of Pleasure*.

filthy

talk

for

troubled

times

Neil LaBute

filthy
talk
for
troubled
times

and other plays

Soft Skull Press / NEW YORK

Library of Congress Cataloging-in-Publication Data

LaBute, Neil
    Filthy talk for troubled times : and other plays / Neil LaBute.
        p. cm.
    ISBN 978-1-59376-282-7 (alk. paper)
    I. Title
    PS3612.A28F55 2010
    812'.6--dc22

                                        2010004019

Cover design by Charlotte Strick
Interior design by Gretchen Achilles
Printed in the United States of America

SOFT SKULL PRESS
An Imprint of Counterpoint LLC
2117 Fourth Street
Suite D
Berkeley, CA 94710

www.softskull.com
www.counterpointpress.com

Distributed by Publishers Group West

10 9 8 7 6 5 4 3 2 1

They fuck you up, your mum and dad,
They may not mean to, but they do.

—PHILIP LARKIN

Sin is the writer's element.

—FRANÇOIS MAURIAC

How did I get here?

—TALKING HEADS

FOR MUM AND DAD

contents

preface

I don't love the idea of going back. Not in time, not to see a movie for a second viewing, and not even into a store again to get the correct change. I'm a bit of a shark that way: swim forward or die.

I do go back all the time, though, when it comes to my plays, so I guess I'm a bit of a liar. That, in fact, may be the least of my sins. I tinker with these things endlessly, and not just for new productions but because they're on my computer and I get bored easily. I'll find myself on a plane writing a new ending for *Fat Pig* or an extra monologue for "Adam" in *The Shape of Things*. A short story based on a short play that came from an idea I had while writing *This Is How It Goes*. Sometimes these tidbits are used by other directors or myself when tackling a new production, but more often than not they simply sit in a file somewhere, the immediate result of my ever-active imagination. In preparing the main play in this volume for publication, I took a much longer look backward than usual— nearly two decades. *Filthy Talk for Troubled Times* came out of my graduate work in Kansas, a collection of scenes and monologues that now seem clearly influenced by everyone from Mr. Mamet to Mr. Shepard to my dad when he had a few drinks in him. Wallace Shawn is in there, too, and I hope a bit of Christopher Durang (I used to eat his work for breakfast), and probably a dozen others. It was around this time that I had discovered the modern English playwrights as well, and their freewheeling sense of structure was a big part of my creative life at the time, so a quick tip of the hat to Barker-Bond-Brenton-Churchill-Hare-Pinter-Storey-et al. is necessary. And yet there is the obvious beginning of a "me" stuffed in there also, if only in the margins. Actually, many of the same themes that I continue to write about today—betrayal, gender politics, the isolation of the individual even in close-knit groups, the numbing death that is the workplace, etc.—are represented in this early work. I also still find a lot of it funny and even a little bit true. It was the first play of mine that got some regional attention, and productions would pop up all around the country during the years that followed. I didn't make a lot of money from it, but it was the play that made me start to feel like a writer.

For better or worse, in terms of both form and content, this is the beginning of Neil LaBute as you might know him today. I continue to love the monologue form you see used here, as well as nameless characters whose dialogue runs roughshod over one another. And I like to cannibalize my own writing. So careful readers might note the joke that was lifted directly out of this play and dropped into the mouth of Aaron Eckhart in the film *In the Company of Men*. Another piece—one I didn't include here—became the text for the only short film I've ever directed, called *Tumble* (if you are dying to see it you'll find it—where else?—on YouTube, featuring Mr. Eckhart's body and my voice). *Filthy Talk for Troubled Times*, then, is a kind of headwaters for me, the ground zero of what I've tried to accomplish throughout the course of my career (or at least during the period that anyone's been paying attention). If nothing else, I still think it's a hell of a title. And it's for these reasons alone (and the fact that someone once yelled "Kill the playwright!" at me during a production in New York—my Off-Off-Broadway debut, no less) that you should get the chance to read it or perform it or to at least add it to the recycling bin in your laundry room.

The other, shorter works that make up the rest of this collection are a series of scenes and monologues—see? I haven't changed much—that have been written and performed in the last few years. A few of them have been completed for benefits or festivals (the non-gender-specific *Romance* grew out of the Sala Beckett theater during a workshop with actors in Barcelona), but most just came to me as ideas and got written because that's my job and my passion. To write. They don't always arrive with a home, these smaller plays, but the ideas seem good at the time and I am my own boss so I sit down and type them out. I've had the great luck of fine productions and terrific actors taking on these jobs, but each of the shorter pieces are, I hope, also interesting to look at in the context of the earlier, longer work as well. In them, you'll see that my setting of choice (a couple of people sitting at a table) hasn't changed much over the years, nor has my penchant for seemingly normal conversations that veer off into the perverse or the unknown. Life is funny and beautiful and weird and I'm here to try to capture some of that on paper. I am an amateur, unfortunately, so I miss a lot of the really gruesome and horrible bits, but hey, I'll keep on trying. After all, it only takes one tsunami on CNN or an Austrian father with a knack for building underground dwellings to blow my macabre or slightly sinister little tales right out of the water.

In the end, fiction is frighteningly normal when reality decides to rear its ugly head.

filthy

talk

for

troubled

times

production history

Filthy Talk for Troubled Times had its world premiere in February 1990 at the Westside Dance Project in New York City in a production directed by Neil LaBute.

Previous versions of this text—under the same title—were presented at various regional locations, beginning with the University of Kansas in 1988.

characters

WAITRESS 1   a woman in her twenties
WAITRESS 2   a woman in her thirties
MAN 1   a man in his thirties
MAN 2   a man in his twenties
MAN 3   a man in his thirties
MAN 4   a man in his twenties
MAN 5   a man in his thirties

setting

A local topless bar (out near the airport).

time

Not so long ago.

NOTE: The monologues and scenes in this play can be shuffled and/or reduced given the abilities and requirements of a given cast or production. It could be played with as few as three actors and one actress with obvious cuts made to accommodate this. Any questions about altering the text must be sent to the author, care of the Gersh Agency in New York City.

Silence. Darkness.

*Lights up slowly to reveal five men huddled in small pockets
around a bar and various tables. Two topless cocktail waitresses
move about them, silently filling orders and cleaning up.*
After a brief tableau, MAN 2 *moves to* WAITRESS 1. *Speaks quietly in
her ear.*

WAITRESS 1   (*to* MAN 2) . . . no, I don't think so.
MAN 2 *moves back to his place near* MAN 1.

MAN 2   Fuck 'em.
MAN 1   Right . . . fuck 'em.

*The other waitress looks down at the filthy table before her. There
is no tip.*

WAITRESS 2   Fuck 'em.

MAN 4 *makes an obscene gesture at an unseen person.*

MAN 4   Fuck 'em.

MAN 3 *responds.*

MAN 3   Fuck 'em, yeah . . . you bet.

MAN 5 *looks around the room with disgust.*

MAN 5   Fuck 'em. Definitely . . . fuck *them*!

Long silence. MAN 1 *glances over at* WAITRESS 1.

MAN 1   . . . all right! So you found her attractive . . . big fucking
    deal, right?
MAN 2   Sure. But I'm not gonna let my guard down, correct?

MAN 1 No chance in hell. Fuck, you let slip you admire the bitch, you're picking out nursery wallpaper next week . . .

MAN 2 . . . hey, nothing wrong with being conservative.

WAITRESS 2 (*overlapping*) . . . tell me this isn't true. If we could get one really good penis—I mean, take turns keeping it in our freezers, bring it out at parties, that kind of thing—fuck, we could do away with men entirely!

MAN 5 (*overlapping*) . . . shit, it's not like I'm dying to meet somebody. I mean, with all this new data they're throwing at us, science says I'm sleeping with like, everybody she's screwed in the last five, maybe ten, years. So if she's at all promiscuous . . . Fuck, that makes me a *fag*! (*Beat.*) I mean, at least in theory . . .

MAN 3 (*overlapping*) . . . but if she *invites* me in, okay.

MAN 4 That's it, huh?

MAN 3 Fuck yes . . . I mean, I don't expect anything for buying dinner, springing for a movie, shit like that . . .

MAN 4 Yeah, that's low-class . . .

MAN 3 But some chick, she lets me in the front door? Then hey, I figure it's open season . . .

MAN 4 Seems reasonable.

MAN 3 Otherwise, she's a tease, right? Now, I can see making clear on the porch she's a prude bitch, doesn't go in for all the humping and what have you—in fact, I kinda admire that— then it's a handshake and "I will see you soon." Fine. (*Beat.*) I never call the gash again so long as I live, but fine . . .

MAN 4 . . . that I can handle . . .

MAN 3 Right. But if it's over on the couch . . . "Is there a late movie on? I've got a nice Chablis . . . " Shit like that . . . (*Beat.*) Fuck it, the bitch is mine.

MAN 4 I get that.

MAN 3 Yep. The way I see it . . . she opens one door, she opens 'em all.

WAITRESS 1 (*overlapping*) . . . I mean, what is going on out there? Huh? Honestly. It's safer in here—with my tits out and all of these guys around—than it is out on the street these days. And I'm being completely serious . . .

Neil LaBute

Long silence.

WAITRESS 1 *crosses the room, taking a drink order from the men.*
They watch her in turn.

MAN 2   Would you look at that . . .

MAN 4   . . . bitch over there?

MAN 3   I wonder if she's . . .

MAN 5   . . . wearing anything under that skirt?

She exits. MAN 1 *watches her leave with contempt.*

MAN 1   . . . ahh, who cares? Fuck 'em all.

The men return to their cabals for more private conversation.

Brief tableau: bar lights fade down as MAN 3 *is highlighted (each*
pocket of conversation will be illuminated one after the other as
the evening moves along).

MAN 3 *sits at the bar.*

MAN 3   . . . fine then, I'm not gonna lie to you . . . it scares me
shitless. Hey, I don't look forward to sprouting lesions down at
the free clinic because some loose-bummed eunuch screwed
the friend of a friend somewhere down the line . . . That's not
fair. I never did anything to him . . . not unless I was pretty
drunk! (*Laughs.*) I'm kidding . . . but AIDS is some spooky
shit, don't you think?

Pause.

MAN 3   Still . . . I'll do whatever I can to help. Answer phones,
collect money at shopping malls, knock on doors, whatever.
Put me down for it. And why? Because it's an "issue," and
issues are important, so, whatever they need . . .

Pause.

MAN 3   I just wish people'd do me one favor: don't try and tell me that Rock Hudson was queer, okay? I mean, I'll sit and look at their charts and filmstrips for weeks . . . That's fine. Just don't say that about Rock. You ever see him in *Pillow Talk* . . . with Doris Day? You know he was fucking her offscreen . . . Come on! Had to be . . . How about *Giant*? There's a great movie . . . and you wanna sell me the notion that Hudson'd rather be popping little Jimmie Dean rather than ol' Liz Taylor? I say go fuck yourself . . .

Pause.

MAN 3   Hey . . . you must've at least watched an episode of *McMillan & Wife*, right? Well, you see it . . . it's still on cable . . . and I'm saying there's no way that McMillan ever got down on his knees for some other guy—if you knew anything about that character you'd know that Hudson just did not have that in him!

 Pause.

MAN 3   I'll be glad to do what I can to help . . . but that's where I draw the fucking line.

MAN 2 *stands with* MAN 1.

MAN 2   . . . where the hell is she?
MAN 1   Who?

Pause.

MAN 2   I don't know . . . haven't met her yet.

MAN 4 *stands talking to* MAN 5.

MAN 4   . . . look, I'm not saying it's for everybody . . . right? Overall, pushing shoes for a living is a gigantic pile of shit . . . no question. I am, however, suggesting an alternative reality here . . . offering up a few of its advantages.

Pause.

MAN 4   Yes, sure, there's the low pay, hustling for commissions . . . fine, agreed, that's bullshit. And yeah, some old cunt staggers in with her fucking gams shoved down in boots she's been traipsing around the mall in all day . . . frankly, the stench makes my balls crawl up in my throat . . . no man deserves that. And . . . there are those days when you're sitting on that stool tying a pair of Buster Browns on some screaming preschool bitch or helping one of those poor crippled fucks find a reasonable-looking gimp shoe—you know, with the big heel and the soft insole—that kind of thing. Times like that, you figure . . . fuck, life as I know it is over.

Pause.

MAN 4   But then . . . suddenly . . . it happens. A fucking miracle transpires. (*He savors this thought a moment.*) I'll be helping one of the usuals, like I said, and I will happen to glance over, very casual, into the mirror next to me . . . occasionally I'll score a little pantie action or a touch of thigh . . . and . . . shit, there it is. My reason for living this otherwise very fucked existence.

Pause.

MAN 4   Some broad . . . maybe thirty, thirty-five . . . still firm is the point I am making here . . . She's sitting back in one of our captain's chairs with a leg up on the shoe bench. I mean, she has the right, doesn't she? It's a big fucking mall, kids are really chapping her ass with their whining . . . So she's

sitting there, waiting for one of our lazy high school pricks
to get her some sandals or something . . . and, I mean,
she's really relaxing, so if I lean down just enough and the
light is with me—yes, certain factors are key—but if things
are working in my favor . . . shit, I can see all the way to
Antarctica! I could just reach over and plant my territorial flag
. . . I mean, fuck, I am right there! Ohhh . . . no briefs,
nothing. Nothing but snatch. (*He smiles.*) Snatch a la mode . . .

Pause.

MAN 4   So I'm sitting there, minding my own business, playing
my natural part in the food chain, as it were . . . and I swear
to God, I'm starting to see, like, daylight coming up from down
there! And why is this? Because . . . this bitch has got her
mouth open and she's smiling . . . right at me. She smiles,
and she's creating a natural shaft of sorts . . . sunlight is just
streaming through!

Pause.

MAN 4   Fuck . . . drop my shoehorn, snap a lace . . . whatever.
Lose the sale, tough shit! She's got me now; I'm in for the
ride on this one. She moves a bit, arches the back a touch,
for effect . . . and I'm not kidding you, she's starting to prism
down there . . . I mean, it's a fucking rainbow. This cannot
be happening! I look up . . . the smile. I look down . . . the
sun sets in the west . . . I look up again . . . she's still got
that grin on her face! So . . . I smile the fuck back until
she's halfway out to the car. Then . . . I stroll back into the
stockroom and get down on my knees—I don't care who's
watching—and I give thanks for being gainfully employed. I
mean, a guy sees a vista like that one . . . he's gotta have
faith that a greater being than himself is running this show.
You know?

Neil LaBute

WAITRESS 2 *stops at a table, wiping it with a rag.*

WAITRESS 2   . . . yep. He was a real fucker, that one . . . I mean, a first-class, cock-sucking piece of shit . . . fucker! You bet he was . . .

Pause.

WAITRESS 2   I mean, he was a . . . well, he wasn't totally fucked, I guess . . . but he was a prick. Treated me like shit! Oh yeah . . . a real prick sandwich, he was, no doubt about it. I mean, he could . . . well, at best he was a true son of a bitch. That much I know . . . I mean, some bitch, somewhere, is plenty proud to call him "son." Trust me . . .

Pause.

WAITRESS 2   Bastard! Yeah . . . that's more like it. That rolls off the tongue more freely when I picture him. He was a complete bastard! I mean . . .

Pause.

WAITRESS 2   Well, he . . . he was not very *nice*. Okay? I don't care what you say. He wasn't very, ahh . . . I mean . . .

Pause.

WAITRESS 2   What the fuck *do* I mean? I mean . . . (*Beat.*) Well, shit, I dunno! But you see what I'm getting at, don't you?

MAN 1 *talking to* MAN 4.

MAN 1   . . .So these gals just think I'm gonna hump their legs like some fucking mongrel, anytime they want . . . right there in the office. Whatever moves them, you know? Like I just need it all times of the day, can't make it till we're back at my place . . . don't have the fucking decency that God'd give a two-legged creature or something, right? (*Beat.*) Got a touch a color blindness . . . Doesn't make me a sons-a-bitching shar-pei, does it?

Pause.

MAN 1   I could see it coming, once I got that dog food account—which is so shitty, I mean, nobody wants to push those fucking "puppy chunks," it's our worst seller—it's simply the fact that I'm now in this huge position of control. Ever since I moved up I've had the whole junior staff scratching at my office door like they were in heat . . .

Pause.

MAN 1   I'll tell you something: you can try and measure success all you want—buy the "beamer," fly first class, whatever—but you're wasting your time. If you're a guy and you achieve any kind of plateau in your career . . . power just rolls out from between your legs like f–ing cologne, and the iciest twat in the place—bitch who wouldn't tell you the building's on fire eight months ago—she's down there at your feet with the rest of 'em . . . digging for scraps.

Pause.

MAN 1   Here . . . lemme give you a piece of advice on how to survive in the world of business. The best way I've found of staying on top of these ladder-licking animals . . . simple. You let them come around all they want—one at a time, you can't take on the whole pack at once, right?—then, let her roll over on her side there, like the poor stupid bitch she is, all warm and inviting . . . and right when she's making her move, all squatted down there like an asshole on her hindquarters . . . you lift your leg and shit in her face! (*Beat.*) Believe me, she'll get the point.

Pause.

MAN 1 Hey, it's not pretty . . . but when you're working with executives, it's effective as hell.

MAN 5 *and* MAN 2 *stand at the bar.*

MAN 5 . . . this is fucked!

MAN 2 What's that?

MAN 5 Look at all the guys here tonight! There's as many men as there are chicks! . . .

MAN 2 I know it . . .

MAN 5 These bitches . . . they really got it figured, don't they? It's like . . . all I see at work is pussy . . . I'm just about the only guy left in my division, practically . . . I mean it. It's like a traveling poon-tang exhibit! 'Course, what good is it? Can't touch a fucking one of 'em.

MAN 2 Yeah, those business things never work out . . .

MAN 5 No shit . . . but they're everywhere! And some of those rags are making maybe upwards of twenty, twenty-five thousand now . . . a year! And I mean every year . . .

MAN 2 Yeah? Well, I suppose if they . . .

MAN 5 And I'm talking about more than one! Shit, these women execs are all over the place! Like fucking cockroaches . . . (*Beat.*) But okay, fine, equal rights, women's lib, fine . . . For women today, sitting in an office is the new masturbation. So be it. I don't wanna get off on a tangent here—but hey, seriously, what is the deal? I come here and I gotta stare at guys' asses all night? Where do all the career gals come dinnertime? They gotta eat, don't they? Gotta have a drink sometime . . . fuck somebody . . . I mean, they're human, after all. Pretty much. But look at this! There are easily an equal number of guys floating around the place tonight . . . It's at least fifty-fifty . . . that like . . . ummmm . . .

MAN 2 Ahh, one to one . . .

MAN 5   Right! What the fuck kind of ratio is that? I'm a single guy . . . so, how's this work, I get one shot the entire night? Who wrote those fucking rules, I'd like to know . . .

Pause.

MAN 5   And that's if all goes perfectly. No snags of any kind— but what if a set of twins stumble in here off the street? Huh? What about those two guys? What then? I suppose it cuts me out a little more, right? What am I standing at then, maybe three-tenths of a fuck? . . . Tit and maybe a handful of pubic hair . . . Fuck that! I'm throwing my money away being here tonight! I'm paying eight-fifty a pop on drinks to not even get a one-snatch minimum? I'm outta here.

He starts off.

MAN 2   Hey . . .

MAN 5   Yeah, what?

MAN 2   Well . . . uhh, what if the twins are girls? I mean, you might end up with both of them, right? Maybe. And that'd be . . . two. At least that would be something. I'm just saying "maybe." It could happen . . .

Pause.

MAN 5   You know, I like the way you think . . . very optimistic. Okay, I'll buy us another round, see what happens . . . and, listen, if any women come by, let me do the talking . . . okay? I know how to handle these things . . .

WAITRESS 1 *stands alone. Stacking glasses.*

WAITRESS 1   . . . okay . . . I'm gonna stand right here . . . you stand still, you're a better target, right? I'll stay right here, and the next guy that comes by . . . I'm gonna talk to him. I mean, really talk. Communicate.

Pause.

WAITRESS 1   I just wanna reach out . . . make some contact,
   you know? A signal, that is all I need. A verbal sign that
   rises up—and this is important—not just between a man
   and woman, but simply . . . us as human beings. Two like
   creatures reaching out and saying, "Hey, I'm here. For God's
   sake, I'm here! I'm alive!"

Pause.

WAITRESS 1   And if that works into dinner and a movie, well then
   . . . it's fate.

Pause. MAN 2 *moves past. She looks at him, then turns to look
away. Awkwardly, he walks slowly off.*

WAITRESS 1   Okay . . . the next guy who comes by, *he's* the one. I
   mean it . . .

MAN 3 *sitting alone.*

MAN 3   . . . fuck.

He contemplates this.

MAN 3   What's the matter with that word, anyway? "Fuck." You
   say it to somebody, they're usually offended as hell. Well,
   fuck . . . at least I had the courtesy to say something.

MAN 4 *stands in a corner of the room.*

MAN 4   . . . I just refuse to believe that women could ever find
   me repulsive . . . It's a mind-set, I guess, but I know I'm
   correct in thinking this . . .

Pause.

MAN 4 And if, perchance, one does—well then, fuck her. There's more where she came from . . . trust me.

MAN 5 *sits alone.*

MAN 5 . . . fuck it, that's it . . . one more person smiles at me, I'm gonna kick some ass . . .

Pause.

MAN 5 This is not a fucking game . . . You wanna smile, do it on your own time! You wanna fuck, pull up a chair . . .

MAN 4 *chats with* MAN 2.

MAN 4 . . . huh? "Silence equals death?" Bullshit! "Silence" is not speaking out loud. (*Beat.*) "Death" is letting some guy put his thing up your ass, right?

Pause.

MAN 4 I mean, a person comes down with a cancer, some kind of Lou Gehrig's disease . . . hey, let's get Jerry Lewis out there, hustling for money . . . I am with you. But some dude is walking around after sex and he's got shit all over his dick, I figure he's pretty much on his own. (*Beat.*) And I don't think that's so cold . . .

WAITRESS 2 *stands talking with* WAITRESS 1.

WAITRESS 2 . . . shit. He really just bent me over, and I don't mean in the good sense . . .

Pause.

Neil LaBute

WAITRESS 2   I guess I opened myself up for it, but you figure . . . just . . . it stands to reason, doesn't it, that eventually things have gotta click? I mean, they can't *all* be motherfuckers! Can they?

Pause.

WAITRESS 2   God . . . who in the fuck goes to the trouble, huh? Why not say, "Fuck off! Leave me alone!" Maybe I'd respect him more. I'm with the guy seven months, no questions, not any pushing—I learned my lesson with that shit years ago—and so, Sunday, he buys a ring, takes me to dinner, and gives me the thing—and this was not shitty quality, it was a gem cluster, that had to cost something—so . . . what? What happened? I mean, I fucking paused for a second, a split second! I'm in my thirties, for chrissakes, a marriage proposal takes a minute to register, you know? Then . . . so he grabs it back, says, "Actually, I've reconsidered. We should stop seeing one another . . . it'd be best. I've met someone . . . " *What?* Is this a fucking joke?! Could he really be that . . . evil? I mean, you don't just do that . . . that kind of hurt takes planning, he had to wanna hurt me . . . right?

Pause.

WAITRESS 2   Bastard! There's an unwritten law, isn't there? You don't even talk about weddings, shit like that, unless it's all the way. You just don't . . .

Pause.

WAITRESS 2   So . . . you can imagine, I'm reeling by this time, fucking crying right there in the restaurant . . . shit . . . I'm a mess. And he tells me to "take it easy." Easy! Here's a guy I'm all ready to take a blood test with and he says I'm making a scene . . . Well, I have this funny way of being hurt when I find out my steady is banging a teenager from his Intro to Lit class . . . I'm silly that way. Anyway, there I am, weeping in my soup . . . this one's gonna hurt, I could feel it . . . and then he leans close, pats me on the head . . . says he'll cover the move-out, wants to pay for my new utilities, everything—and "can we still see each other . . . dinner?" (*She takes a quick drink.*) My hand just shot out . . . even thinking back, I don't think I could've controlled it—maybe—but I didn't let go of his balls until he passed out in his salad. (*Beat.*) I just kept turning 'em, full revolutions, like the whole scrotum would come free if I just worked on it awhile—for a minute there, I thought I could feel the fuckers giving way, I really did!—but I couldn't get 'em to come off . . .

Pause.

WAITRESS 2   You know, for all the stink guys make about 'em, those little bastards are pretty solid. (*Beat.*) Too bad, I could've used something to remember him by . . .

MAN 3 *stands with* MAN 5. *They watch* MAN 2 *pass by.*

MAN 3   . . . fuck, I'm glad I'm a guy! You know?
MAN 5   Yeah, why's that?

Pause.

MAN 3   . . . because then I don't have to date 'em.

MAN 1 *talking to* MAN 4.

MAN 1   . . . and I was going into the racquet club—this was a couple months ago—and out comes this couple . . . regular people, sweats and whatnot on . . . but the breeze is pretty solid and so one of them, the woman, turns her face away from the wind, toward me . . . and I'm staring into the eyes of death, I swear to God! I mean, give this bitch a *scythe* and just save her some time, I'm not kidding you! This is deathbed material here . . .

Pause.

MAN 1   Oh, no question she had it. (*Beat.*) Absolutely none . . . Her eyes are, like, blinking "HIV" in Morse code to me! Seriously . . . but I smiled at her. I did. And you know what? (*He smiles.*) Her face lit up, Jesus . . . you'd've thought I was Jonas Salk or something, the smile that just suddenly appears. And I felt good about that. I did . . . It was just my . . . tiny bid for *humanity.* You know?

Pause.

MAN 1   But: the whole time—and this only took a few seconds, but all while we were passing—I wasn't thinking "humanitarian gesture, reach out to my fellow creatures" crap. No. I'm noticing that her hair is wet, and now I'm trying to figure out if she used the hot tub, the ice plunge, or what. Same old me. (*Beat.*) Anyway, I shot baskets for maybe twenty minutes and then went home.

Pause.

MAN 1   What do you think? I showered at my place . . .

MAN 5 *sits and talks.*

MAN 5   . . . so this buddy of mine, and I'm—before I say this I should mention that we were all pretty stoned at the time— but me and a few guys I know . . . we caught these two gays in the park one night, and they were fucking. Yeah. Not even very late, middle of this neighborhood, over near the kiddie slide. Seriously.

Pause.

MAN 5   So this friend—he's really a nut—he sneaks over to 'em, motions the rest of us to come with him, and suddenly, we, like, jump 'em and we pin these buttfuckers down. And he . . . well, he starts screwing the one on top, right? Seriously, guy drops his pants and—so we're all rolling around on the grass, holding these two down—the one on the bottom reveals himself to be this fucking *Chinese* dude—don't know what the fuck's going through the other queer's mind, stooping that low—but we're holding 'em down, and my buddy's forcing the guy on top, who is now in the middle—it was confusing when it was happening, too—but he's making this son of a bitch hump the Chink underneath while he rides this top guy. I mean, the middle guy. Well, you know what I mean! Can you believe that?!

Pause.

MAN 5   Both these fags are weeping now, I mean, fucking gasping for air by the time it was over, but he just kept doing it anyway, our friend does . . . screaming at 'em, "That'll teach ya! That'll teach ya!" (*Beat.*) This guy *really* gets wired when he smokes . . .

Pause.

MAN 5   Anyway, I don't know what the *fuck* he thought he was teaching 'em . . . but it's still, you know, a pretty interesting story.

WAITRESS 2 *stands talking with* WAITRESS 1.

WAITRESS 2   . . . I kid you not . . . he stood there and called me a cunt. Figure that one out . . .

Pause.

Neil LaBute

WAITRESS 2   "Cunt" . . . why is it that there are no verbal
equivalents to the degrading . . . scatological . . . slang
that men use on us? Hmmm? You know as well as I do
that anything we fire off at them pales compared to the
ammunition they have . . . right at their fingertips . . . "Dick,"
"cock," "prick" . . . What are those compared to "slash," or
"gash"? Ohh, and . . . what about "slit"? Huh? And, trust me,
this is far from a comprehensive list . . .

Pause.

WAITRESS 2   Listen to those words! God, they are hateful . . .
violence-oriented . . . Hell, they've even got better consonant
groupings than ours do! It is a real shame when we can't
even keep up in a fucking name-calling contest! And the thing
is, if you look at the words they use, and I mean, really *study*
'em, they apply to men much more readily than they do to us.
(*Smiles.*) Listen, I speak from experience when I say . . . just
because some man doesn't *have* one does not necessarily
mean that he can't *be* one.

Pause.

WAITRESS 2   Right? I mean . . . shit, look at that guy over there:
now he's a *cunt* if ever I saw one. He just doesn't know it
yet . . .

MAN 4 *sits talking.*

MAN 4   . . . trust me. You can tell when some bitch wants you. I
am not kidding, you really can . . . something . . . in her eyes,
maybe a touch of whisper in her "could you pass the salt?"
Could be anything, but it'll be there . . . *if* she wants you.
(*Beat.*) There's always some telltale flicker when they really
mean it. You just gotta watch for it . . . keep your eyes open.

Pause.

MAN 4 'Course . . . it's a hell of a lot easier if she just walks up and says, "Why don't I slip you out of those jeans and spin around on your dick like a fucking Christmas ornament?"

Pause.

MAN 4 But, hey, you can't count on that, so it's best to plan ahead . . .

MAN 3 *sits with* MAN 2.

MAN 3 . . . but what if the bitch gives me a disease? Huh?

Pause.

MAN 3 Well, fuck . . . I guess it's better than leaving her phone number. I mean, *penicillin's* one thing, but ringing me up all hours and *chatting* . . . that's where this shit gets messy.

WAITRESS 1 *stands alone.*

WAITRESS 1 "Commitment" . . . com-mit-ment. Hearing that word come out of my mouth used to mean so much to me . . .

Pause.

WAITRESS 1 Now it just means that when some guy wants to sleep with me *and* one of my friends . . . I promise to make it sound like it was *my* idea.

MAN 1 *stands at the bar.*

MAN 1 . . . you know, I have never cheated on any woman . . . I mean, that I've had a serious—and I'm emphasizing *serious* here, but—a serious relationship with. *Ever.*

Pause.

MAN 1 Well . . . at least not that first night . . .

MAN 3 *sits talking with* **MAN 4**.

MAN 3 . . . and I don't mean this in a degrading way.
MAN 4 Right . . .
MAN 3 I'm just offering it as an exhibit . . . a truth . . . a manifesto, if you will, of unbiased insight. See?
MAN 4 Okay. But what the fuck's your point?
MAN 3 I'm just saying . . .
MAN 4 Yeah?
MAN 3 . . . that as a basic fact . . .
MAN 4 Okay . . .
MAN 3 . . . the male member's better than the female. That's all I'm saying. And I'm not implying "better" in the sense of "better than" . . . not specifically, not in the physical sense, or mentally, or even religiously, although I personally do believe there is a slight spiritual advantage, or edge, if you will, to the male member. (*Beat.*) Honestly . . . the female is inferior.
MAN 4 So, you're saying . . . what? The male member is *superior*?
MAN 3 Right. But in no way do I want to start a thing here, a scene of any kind. Too fucking easy . . .
MAN 4 Okay, but . . .
MAN 3 I just wanna entertain this idea, no more than a germ of a thought, really . . . a *nugget*, but I think it holds true . . . the greatness of the . . .
MAN 4 . . . male member?
MAN 3 Right.
MAN 4 Member? Hmm . . .
MAN 3 Exactly.
MAN 4 Member of what? What the fuck's the guy a member of?
MAN 3 Excuse me?
MAN 4 What're we talking about here . . . is this a ball club or something?

filthy talk for troubled times

MAN 3 Oh. No . . . I'm not referring to "it" as a "he" . . . I'm making "it" an "it" . . . spade a spade, really. *The* male member—actual appendage.

Silence.

MAN 4 What're you . . . you're not talking about some guy's thing?

MAN 3 Right . . .

MAN 4 His *dick*?

MAN 3 Well . . . yes. His member, or penis. Whichever you prefer.

MAN 4 Ahh, I don't prefer anything . . . What're we talking about fucking *joints* for? Who the fuck is this guy?

MAN 3 No one, actually . . . just a hypothetical figure.

MAN 4 . . . well, I don't wanna . . .

MAN 3 I'm just suggesting this, and only in the broadest terms—as a thing, simply as an entity unto itself . . . the male member is greater than the female. (*Beat.*) . . . You see what I'm shooting for here? Just a kind of very open-ended thesis . . . something we can springboard from. Scientifically.

MAN 4 A thesis . . . about some guy's dick?

MAN 3 Right. Although it needn't be an actual dick . . . or member . . . of someone we know. As I stated earlier. That's the beauty of this whole concept . . . it's universal!

MAN 4 We're talking about . . . what? All the guys' . . . joints in the world? *Every*body?

MAN 3 Sure. All-encompassing. But again, only in the most polite, self-deprecating terms . . . This is not meant to drive a fucking wedge between the sexes!

Pause. MAN 4 *considers this.*

MAN 4 So you're saying that a guy's dick . . .

MAN 3 . . . but again, very politely . . .

MAN 4 Okay, but . . . you're *politely* saying that a guy's penis . . .

MAN 3 Or member . . . they're synonymous, really . . .

Neil LaBute

MAN 4   A guy's . . . fuck . . . "member" . . . is better than some
        lady's?
MAN 3   Correct. All things being equal, the male member comes
        out the big winner.

Pause.

MAN 4   Okay. I can see that.
MAN 3   Sure. It's simple . . .
MAN 4   What you're *really* saying . . .
MAN 3   . . . just suggesting . . .
MAN 4   . . . is that the dick would kick some ass! If we compared
        the two.
MAN 3   Well . . . yes. It would certainly distinguish itself . . .
MAN 4   That I can believe!

Silence. MAN 3 *about to say something. Stops. Thinks.*

MAN 3   Trouble? What?
MAN 4   In theory . . . I'm seeing a practical problem. My problem
        is . . . and this, I believe, is across the board . . .
MAN 3   Yes?
MAN 4   Women . . . don't have 'em.

Pause.

MAN 3   Mmmmm . . .
MAN 4   See what I mean? How can you compare the two when . . .
MAN 3   Still, I believe comparisons could be drawn . . .
MAN 4   How?
MAN 3   I'm speaking of *broad* parallels, of course . . . but certain
        factors are still undeniable.
MAN 4   Like what?
MAN 3   Well . . .
MAN 4   Guys got 'em and women don't. Now, sure . . . they got
        that other thing, their snatch, vagina . . . you know . . .
MAN 3   . . . their *member* . . .

filthy talk for troubled times   25

MAN 4   But it's not . . . is it? Not really. It's different . . .

MAN 3   How so?

MAN 4   Well, fuck, I dunno . . . I'm shooting from the hip here, but wouldn't "member" connotate an appendage? Kind of a dangling . . . free-hanging sorta thing . . . like a . . . dick?

MAN 3   Or member.

MAN 4   Whatever! Doesn't it?

MAN 3   Well, yes, but I'm speaking in the most generic way. Simply weighing the two . . .

MAN 4   Right, right, but how can you?

MAN 3   What? Taking two like things and holding them up for scrutiny . . .

MAN 4   Yeah, but . . . still . . .

MAN 3   It's only a hypothesis . . .

MAN 4   Look, I see what you're driving at and I admire the effort. I do. All *I'm* saying is that you go ahead and compare this shit all you want to. Eventually, the truth is gonna win out . . .

MAN 3   . . . but . . .

MAN 4   *And* the result of all this is . . .

MAN 3   Fair enough. I'm only interested in end results . . .

MAN 4   The *fact* remains: women do not have dicks. *No* fucking way . . .

Silence.

MAN 3   Okay . . . you got me there.

WAITRESS 1 *stands at the bar.*

WAITRESS 1   . . . but why is it if you give a guy an abortion, then he'll give you the world . . . but if you give him a kid, he gives you the front door?

Pause.

WAITRESS 1   Huh? Now explain that one to me . . .

MAN 4 *and* MAN 5 *stand together.*

MAN 4 . . . but . . . it's . . . (*Beat.*) Awwww, screw it . . . Okay, I give up.

MAN 5 What . . . so easily? I thought you were seriously challenging my theory here . . .

MAN 4 No, you've convinced me. I just . . . *How* the fuck do I get into these conversations?

MAN 5 Come on . . . you can't think of one thing?

MAN 4 Uh-uh . . . I guess you're right. *Every*thing around us is phallic . . .

MAN 5 Fucking right . . . *or* based on the phallic image.

Pause.

MAN 4 You're certain, though? No doubts?

MAN 5 Absolutely none . . .

MAN 4 What about food? I know we touched on some things, but all food?

MAN 5 You shitting me? *Any*thing. Pasta, bananas. Whole cucumber family.

MAN 4 And candy? Children's candy?

MAN 5 You take a long, hard look at a Tootsie Roll sometime and then we'll talk, okay? (*Beat.*) So?

MAN 4 Umm, shit . . . just choose something?

MAN 5 Sure . . .

MAN 4 Ahh . . . okay, bacon?

MAN 5 It comes in pretty *long* strips . . .

MAN 4 Oh yeah. Fine, what about yams?

MAN 5 I take it that you've never seen a fresh yam, then? Can make a woman fucking quiver just to pick one up in the vegetable section . . .

MAN 4 Okay, fine . . . other store things . . . uhhh, batteries?

MAN 5 Phallic.

MAN 4 Shopping cart?

MAN 5 Phallic.

MAN 4 A mop? Oh, wait, what am I thinking? Of course it is . . . with the handle thingie and . . . the . . .

MAN 5 See how easy this becomes?

MAN 4 No, hold on . . . fuck . . . What about a lobster? Like those lobsters they keep in the tank at the deli section . . . What about . . .

MAN 5 Fuck, even the *tank* they keep them in is phallic! Look at it, it is longer than it is wide—and that's the only standard we can honestly follow, right?

MAN 4 But there's gotta be . . . What about a building? Something like that, huh? With all the varieties of architecture that we've . . .

MAN 5 I don't wanna push this . . . but try to imagine a building that doesn't fall into the phallic category . . . Which way do we build?! Up! *Up!* And if not up, then out. We either go horizontal—which, to be fair, is how our dicks spend a good portion of their waking hours—or we clamber for the stars . . . See? Just like the penis, all things strive to turn their pathetic little heads skyward . . . It's a bit sad, but oh so true . . . It's up or out, right? Things that go down are wrong, frightening . . . Let's face it, just plain *bad.* When the Dow Jones is fucked, where's it go? Down. You gotta eat out a woman's snatch, what'll they say to you? "Go down on me" . . . and I guess we all know that is no fucking treat . . . Hell? It's down . . . fucking Satan, that's what you ultimately find if you keep going down, that or coal mines. You wanna work in a sons-a-bitching *mine*? Of course not, nobody does. *All* these things . . . holes, basements? Shit . . . what good is a basement? Those fuckers flood first sign of rain. You following this? Just use this as a rule of thumb . . . up is good, down is bad. Everything is phallic, any deviations to that idea suck shit . . .

Pause.

MAN 5 Look at us! We are phallic by design . . . and, more than that, by nature. I mean, the world just naturally yearns to be, or become, phallic. What living thing doesn't reach toward

Neil LaBute

the heavens all during its brief stay on earth? Huh? It's a brotherhood . . . It is, even with women. You've heard of "penis envy"? It's the very basis of my argument here! Hey, those with the cocks run this place, let's quit fucking around and admit it!

Pause.

MAN 4 Yeah, maybe you're on to something there . . . 'cause it's . . .

Pause.

MAN 4 Wait! What you said about women . . . What about their private . . . well, you know . . . their privates—fuck it, members—or whatever you wanna call 'em? Huh?
MAN 5 Yeah. So?
MAN 4 Well, think about it . . . you could hardly call that thing "phallic." It's the complete antithesis . . . isn't it? It can't be . . . I mean, shit, there's hardly any fucking *shape* to the thing as it is!

Pause.

MAN 4 Look . . . I just had this argument a little while ago with somebody and I think I'm right in saying this. Okay? Now . . . a woman's genitals can't really be considered phallic. Can they?

Pause.

MAN 5 Hmm . . . maybe not. (*Beat.*) Well, look, with all the phallic shit floating around, we gotta have someplace to put it . . . so maybe *that's* why a gal's crotch is shaped the way it is. You gotta admit, it's not exactly the most enviable design . . . I mean, you ever look up under a woman before? Huh? It's like a fucking *bowling ball* down there . . .

filthy talk for troubled times

MAN 4 Yeah . . . but you do agree, then, a woman—or her shit underneath, anyway—is not phallic . . .

Pause.

MAN 5 Fine. I agree . . . No, you're right. Women, unlike the norm, are not phallic . . .

Silence.

MAN 5 . . . but we fucking make 'em pay for it, don't we?

MAN 3 *and* MAN 2 *sit at a table, lost in discussion.*

MAN 3 . . . and I gotta stop right here and say this whole concept? It springs from a genuine love for the female race . . .
MAN 2 . . . okay . . .
MAN 3 . . . but . . . "women." Huh?
MAN 2 Women.
MAN 3 Right . . . *women!* You can't fucking trust them . . .

Pause.

MAN 2 Why not?
MAN 3 Well . . . personally, I could never trust anything that bleeds for a week and doesn't die . . .

Silence.

MAN 2 Oh. Yeah.

MAN 2 *gets up and crosses near* WAITRESS 1. *He falters, then moves on.*

WAITRESS 1 God, I wish he would stop approaching me! I mean . . . if he's not careful, I'm gonna go to bed with him, and that's the last thing I want tonight!

Pause.

WAITRESS 1   Actually, the last thing I want is to be alone, but . . . the other last thing is to be with someone.

MAN 1 *is talking to* MAN 3 *and* MAN 4.

MAN 1   . . . hey, you can say whatever the hell you want, but I'm here to level with you . . . you guys are floating up to your eyebrows in shit . . . rock and roll has always been full of wimpy-ass fucks, all these guys . . . Jagger, Springsteen. . . Lennon . . . fuck, even Morrison. I'm telling you, no balls on any of them. Like it really takes a big set of brass ones to give it to some pubescent groupie hiding in your shower back in the hotel. Fuck, I do that now, and I'm nobody!

Pause.

MAN 1   You gotta look at the old guys, the Vegas set . . . Now these were men born with their dicks securely fastened between their legs. Am I right? Dean, Jerry, fuck, even little Sammy Davis . . . hey, he might've had a gamey eye, but you point him in the right direction . . . and *bam!* Do not be fooled by these guys. They may be pushing some dopey floor show for a living—you gotta eat, right?—but in their primes, these were *men's* men I'm talking about here.

Pause.

MAN 1   'Course, the king of them all was Frank Sinatra . . . right? Now there was a man. I like that guy! He's a role model . . . and you just know every woman wanted him . . . you can see it. You gotta like Sinatra! And . . . it's not just the voice. Believe me, plenty of guys could sing rings around him. Crosby, Nat King Cole? *Golden* voices—but, and this is the key—just as limp as fucking garden hoses! I don't know what it is, but maybe only every fourth or fifth male singer in the world can get it up. I've actually read about this, freak of nature. Is that odd as hell or not? Most singers—and this has been tested—a hard-on is just not in their repertoire . . .

Pause.

MAN 1   Isn't that amazing? Documented fact . . . a lot of these vocalists just don't have the dick for the job.

Pause.

MAN 1   Nope . . . I will always come round to Sinatra. And like I said, it's not the singing, not the mafia connections . . . that's cool, but no big deal . . . The fact of the matter? The reason I admire the guy? Because he *fucks.*

Pause.

MAN 1   Hey, everything about Sinatra says "fuck" . . . his look, his wives. You gotta like a guy, at his age, who pulls the fucking teething spoon outta Mia Farrow's mouth just to take her down hard a few times . . . huh? And especially, the Sinatra sound. You may find a better voice, I said you could, but Frank's music just . . . "fucks." You know? There's really no better way to describe it . . .

Pause.

MAN 1   You find yourself with some time on your hands, spin a little St. Francis on the stereo . . . Now, you gotta listen close, but in the background, quiet-like, almost subliminal, back near the horn section where all those no-cock singers have a bit of "do-be-do-wop" going down—you listen close. Frank is back there whispering a primal chant to manhood everywhere! He had to be careful, I mean, fuck, even "the voice" had to put up with the censors, right? But he's back there . . . and you know what he's saying? Ol' Frankie's saying, "Hey, don't be an asshole. Get those pants off her and let's fuck!"

Pause.

MAN 1 Ya see what I mean? Sinatra *fucks!* And that is the truth, my friends.

WAITRESS 2 *alone.*

WAITRESS 2 . . . see? It's funny, isn't it? I mean, I just don't follow the guy. It's like, nobody seems to want to have fun anymore. I guess that's what it is now: we're all just too serious. I mean, I'm as fucked up and miserable as the next person, but I don't let it get me down. You know?

Pause.

WAITRESS 2 It just stupefies me . . . Can you understand this mess? I'm just toying with him, having some fun—I was on the rebound at that time from somebody—and I just, teasingly, undo his fly, give his thing a playful slap or two—and he starts bawling and puts his fucking head on my shoulder! Yeah. Figure that. I'm sitting there, naked, and he's loving it, I make this move toward shedding his clothes, and he, like, bursts into tears. What the fuck? So, I did the only sensible thing: I just got up, grabbed my shit, and went outside—I didn't even dress until I got to the bus stop 'cause I'll be damned if I'm gonna put up with that kinda bullshit my first night back dating!

Pause.

WAITRESS 1 Look, I'm plenty happy to get off with some guy right away—hell, it gives us something to talk about—but I am not gonna be his fucking psychologist. Why should I? What'd he ever do for me? Right?

filthy talk for troubled times   33

MAN 5 *sits.*

MAN 5 . . . never did me any fucking good, I'll tell you . . .
seriously. I've been seeing this female shrink for maybe four
years . . . You know where it got me? Huh?

Pause.

MAN 5 Any ideas? A bill for twenty thousand dollars . . . and I
was still waking up with the same shit-sucking headaches
I had since I was a kid . . . So guess what I did? Huh? I
found my own cure . . . started banging that good-for-nothing
Freudian bitch! What the hell, I figured she might scream out
something in bed that she was keeping from me during our
sessions—there was a time I was desperate to try anything—
plus, I figured I was getting a little return on my investment.

Pause.

MAN 5 But, shit, here I'm still suffering while she pulls in the
dough and gets it regular on the side now—she's married,
some guy I never met—try and sort that shit out! The broad
sits in this big chair, very cool, reserved, legs tightly pulled
together . . . listening to me whine about my mom and dad for
an hour a week and telling me to, like, "get in touch with your
feelings . . . don't be so physically motivated." Shit like that
. . . *and* then when my time is up, off comes the dress and
she's over on the couch chewing on my pecker like a fucking
cocker spaniel. So, I ask you, where is the treatment here?
How am I gonna get over my sexual anxieties at this rate? I
am not fucked up, by the way, I just have some questions.
So don't get me wrong. I mean, look, it's not that I mind the
method she's using, it just doesn't seem very scientific, that's
all . . .

Pause.

MAN 5   Still, to be fair, she did knock twenty bucks an hour off of our sessions. Fuck, I know a cheaper rate's not exactly a cure . . . but I figure I'm making progress, right?

MAN 3 *sits with the other men.*

MAN 3   . . . you think I'm *proud* of what I did? Huh? No. *But* at least I am able to stare my mistakes right in the fucking face, okay? Now, you got me started, you wanna hear the end of this or not?

Pause.

MAN 3   All right then . . . shut the fuck up and hear me out . . . So, here I am, forty-five minutes after I delivered this package . . . and this secretary is still pulling me down on the desk for another round of sexual gymnastics! She's roaring through full splits, these aerial twists, unbelievable shit! This bitch is definitely talented . . . a very phenomenal young lady.

Pause.

MAN 3   But, see, she's wasting her affections on me . . . because, fuck, I'm scared! . . . The whole time, I'm trying to get my clothes on, wrapping things up—I'm an errand boy, for chrissakes, I got no business humping this working woman in the middle of her boss's office! And then suddenly, my wallet, it pulls a no-show. Oh, come on, I can't believe this shit! First I get a chance to fuck this . . . Athena—this was a beautiful woman, no more than twenty-two—and now suddenly the gods turn around and take a dump squarely on my head. I mean, where the fuck could my ID be? I've been face-first inside this babe for not even an hour: How far can it get? I know the bitch didn't grab it, she's got nothing on—I make her bend over and check her anyway, which, by the way, she does with relish—but that fucker's disappeared! Goddammit!! So, I start taking the place apart . . . I mean, literally. But no

filthy talk for troubled times   35

luck. Fuck! Now I'm starting to go a bit insane. I mean, there is a fucking *law* office trying to run itself the other side of the door, this lawyer could show from his meeting at any moment . . . and me and this nude typist of his are scrambling about looking for my wallet as if we're the only two people on earth . . . Jesus! Life has a weird way of keeping you guessing.

Pause.

MAN 3   . . . actually, it's funny, though, isn't it? I mean, how one minute this broad is the finest meat I've seen on the planet, next thing you know—at least in my mind—she's a notch below a couple pictures of my brother's wedding. Fuck, once my belongings come up missing, I don't even recall ever looking at the lady again. Seriously. But, you know where I'm coming from here . . . you can't lose your wallet. You know? A wallet is sacred! It's your temple, right? It's not like the stuff inside is of monumental value, but to me the shit in those two leather pockets is my world . . . I had to have it back! So I don't know what to think. I figure it's now anywhere between the warehouse and that gal's thighs, so I better fucking start backtracking! I say a "Thanks!" to the girl, give her my number—it's actually to the shipping room, I don't wanna start something serious here—and I'm outta that place . . .

Pause.

MAN 3   I search for two fucking weeks . . . nothing. Not a goddamn *trace*. So finally, I gotta face this . . . the thing might still be back in that office. Somewhere. I head over there . . . right past the secretary's cubicle—I don't even look in, how's that for fucking cold?—and straight up to the guy's desk on which I had been banging this gal . . .

Pause.

Neil LaBute

MAN 3   And fuck . . . I shit you not, there it is. Sitting right next
to this dude's calendar, stuck through on his note spindle.
Just waiting for me. Okay, he's on to me . . . What'm I gonna
do? Think fast . . . not that I'm scared—you fuck an employee
on a man's ink blotter, I figure you can usually look him in the
eye—so I decide to come clean. I explain the situation to him.
And then . . . he explains it to *me*.

Pause.

MAN 3   My luck! I run up against a queer! Secretary like that and
this guy's looking for dick to suckle on . . . go figure. He says
he likes my style and would I mind a repeat performance,
with a slight variation?—yeah, I'd call a prick up my butt a
variation, if ever I heard one—so, fuck . . . this is not good. I
beg him, I plead. I offer to talk with the girl out front so that
he can at least indulge in some of that, but no dice. Deal is,
my hide for the cowhide or I can get lost . . . that's his offer.
Oh, man, I gotta think this through . . .

Pause.

MAN 3   I look at him . . . Can I just beat the shit outta him? No
chance, I'm just a boy. I glance over at the wallet, but I'm sure
I could never just grab it and dash or you know that would've
been my course of action, I swear to God! I weighed the
consequences heavily. If you learn nothing else about me,
you will find I'm no pushover . . . but I see no way out. It's a
complete no-win! Shit. So, I finally think to myself, "What the
fuck, it's worth it!" You gotta realize, I'm no fag, but he's got
my wallet, for chrissakes! This is my personal property I'm
talking about! I must've had *thirty* bucks in Arby's coupons
alone in there . . . so.

Pause.

filthy talk for troubled times   37

MAN 3 The rest happened in a blur. I undid my belt, dropped my pants—this young exec has his gray dress flannels around his ankles before I could bend over—and I just held on for the ride. And . . . that was that.

He looks at the others.

MAN 3 Fuck you guys . . . no details! (*Beat.*) Trust my better judgment . . . it was none too pretty. I just locked my eyes on that calfskin beauty waiting for me on the desk and made it through . . . I made it! I even used the old coin purse as a bite stick at one point—to keep from crying. Fuck, I'm not ashamed to say it, I almost cried! I've got dignity just like anybody else. Anyway, the point is, my ass healed . . . no harm done . . . and more importantly, I still carry that wallet to this day. I figure, sometimes in this world a guy's got to make a few sacrifices . . . right?

Pause.

MAN 3 Hey, come on . . . don't look at me like that. I told you this was a bit off the beaten path. Fuck, the guy had my wallet . . .

Long silence.

MAN 4 Wow. So . . . did you guys fuck?
MAN 3 What?
MAN 4 You and him . . . did you do it? Like, all the way?
MAN 3 Am I talking to myself here? "Did we do it"?! Take a big, fat fucking guess . . .
MAN 2 It was sort of unclear . . .
MAN 3 . . . I mean, what am I opening up to you guys for, my *health*? I thought I was sharing a pretty incredible example of what a guy will do to protect something he loves . . .
MAN 2 Hey, just asking . . .

Neil LaBute

The other men look at MAN 3. MAN 1 *gets up, moves off.*

MAN 3   Anyway, it's in the past. Besides, who can realistically
    sit here and say he wouldn't have done the same thing?
    Huh? (*Looks at his pals.*) I mean, who here's never had a gay
    experience . . . right? In college, or . . .

Pause.

MAN 3   Oh, come on . . . *really?*

They remain silent or shake their heads in disagreement.

MAN 1 *stands at the bar.*

MAN 1   . . . it just seems like we're approaching this problem ass-
    backwards. I mean, you gotta treat women like anybody else,
    right? They're the same as you or me . . . basically . . . except
    maybe they get to sit down to piss. But that's not really an
    advantage . . . not the way I look at it.

Pause.

MAN 1   And anyhow, in no way should some broad be able to
    use squatting instead of standing as a bargaining chip in
    a relationship . . . She is still a human being. If anything,
    slightly less mobile than we . . . I'm just saying that we can't
    go around making some gal a sex object on account of what
    she is sporting down there. There'll be hell to pay. I'm sure of
    it . . .

Pause.

MAN 1   Nice ass . . . some kind of tits . . . nothing fancy, a
    respectable package . . . Okay! Fine. But what am I gonna do,
    fall down and fucking *die* because she smiles at me in the

produce aisle? Well, perhaps I will, but I'm sure as shit not gonna let her in on it . . .

Pause.

MAN 1 It's a matter of splitting hairs, I suppose, but in my book, women: sex objects . . . no thank you. But, objects of sex . . . now we're getting somewhere. You see?

Pause.

MAN 1 I feel word placement is key to a manageable relationship . . .

WAITRESS 2 *stands speaking to* WAITRESS 1.

WAITRESS 2   . . . oh, sure. I had an orgasm . . . once. I mean, I guess it was an orgasm . . . a muscle in my left thigh twitched. 'Course, I thanked the guy . . . profusely. Otherwise, he never would've shut up, and I had to work in the morning. I really hate that shit . . . like when they feign . . . interest, you know?

Pause.

WAITRESS 2 All this crap about men are trying to be more caring and sensitive . . . bullshit! They can kiss my ass . . . it's the same old business. You can lick 'em until you start to black out, it'd still take a court order to get them down on you. Instead, you're treated to thirty, maybe forty seconds of tit massage . . . thrilling . . . a couple minutes of clumsy humping in some god-awful position—his choice, always— and then you gotta lie there and watch him buck and snort like some rodeo animal for an hour until he falls off to sleep. (*Smiles.*) Ain't love beautiful?

Pause.

Neil LaBute

WAITRESS 2 Then, the topper . . . an elbow to the ribs . . . "Hey, you make it?" Really sensitive, like we've got a fucking recipe for an orgasm! Jesus . . . take my vagina and sew it the fuck closed! Please, do me the favor. This is not my idea of a hot fuck. I mean, I am up to here with these smarmy little one-nighters with some poor, limp CPA. A couple tickets to the Ice Capades, cheap wine back at his place, and then facedown on the bathroom tile for the evening while he dabbles in "something he's never done before . . . " Shit! Give me some romance, for God's sake! Would someone please come along and drop a decent guy right in my lap . . . Can I get some service, please? I don't think it's unreasonable. Some flowers, touch of candlelight . . . What the hell's the matter with a fairy-tale ending? Look, you give me my Prince Charming and don't worry . . . I'll fuck his brains out. So far, though . . . same old shit.

Pause.

WAITRESS 2 Yeah . . . winter of . . . no, I guess it was spring, actually. Spring of '97 . . . I had my orgasm.

MAN 4 *stands near the bar.*

MAN 4 . . . that's right, every time. My women orgasm *every* fucking time. Guaranteed.

Pause.

MAN 4 No, I'm not saying right off . . . What am I, a *magician*? There is the occasional tryst when I gotta stick with a gal for a while . . . Hell, maybe even a day or two. I remember one time . . . Chicago . . . in springtime, I think . . . I was doing this gal for probably thirty hours . . . straight. It is not a fucking lie. No rest . . . always going at it. Hey, it's possible . . . We ordered food up to the room! Sure, the waiter who brought the stuff in saw us pumping away . . . I was just in for a weekender, what the fuck did I care?

Pause.

MAN 4 And to be completely candid, I'm someone who finds it fulfilling to let another guy in on some of the techniques I employ on any given bitch . . . I'm a *samaritan*, I admit it.

Pause.

MAN 4 Seriously . . . thirty hours. But I got her . . . and believe me, that bitch thanked me. *Profusely* . . .

Pause.

MAN 4 It's a matter of control . . . and I take it personally, don't think I don't. Some of them . . . they wanna fight you, make you work for it, then pretend they never got there. Bullshit! I fucking ask them outright . . . "Hey, you make it or not?" Now, they may try and hide it, but if they're honest with themselves, in front of their God: they always orgasm. Every time. *Guaranteed.*

MAN 5 *stands talking.*

MAN 5 . . . hey, that's nothing. Listen . . . Any of you guys ever make it with a gay chick? No, seriously. Like a lesbian or something of a similar nature? Huh? Contrary to popular belief, I hear those bitches are really hot in the sack, you fuck 'em on an "off" night . . . I mean it! Hell, they like to dabble in dick just like a normal gal, don't let that biker getup fool you. See, to them, it's like toying with witchcraft or *necromancy* . . . shit like that. Now, I'm not saying that I understand it completely myself . . . but I guess to a woman whose diet consists mainly of tit and bush . . . you gotta figure that pulling the real thing up outta somebody's boxers is a little

Neil LaBute

like opening Pandora's box! And, trust me, I'm using "box" in an extremely figurative way here . . .

MAN 5 *laughs at his own joke.*

MAN 5   Right? I mean, think of the first time you grabbed it yourself. It's a little bit of a rush, isn't it? 'Course it is! Now, come on, admit it . . . you guys are adults . . . who's wanted to try one just to see if you couldn't turn her around? Huh? Open those queer fucking eyes up a bit, give her a taste of the sweet life—touch of the old "la dolce vita"—you know what I'm saying? Fess up! You know that all those bitches are just using that homo number as a front—it's all "catch me if you can" game-playing bullshit. Correct? And I figure—if you take the time to play some hardball with these chicks— couple of them are gonna come on over to our side . . . it's the fucking law of averages!

Pause.

MAN 5   So, come on, now . . . I'm looking for honesty here: Who's ever wanted to tangle with a lesbian? Be truthful!

He waits with his hand held high. No hands from anybody else. Slowly MAN 5 *drops his arm down.*

MAN 5   Well . . . fuck, me either! I was just curious, that's all.

WAITRESS 1 *sits.*

WAITRESS 1   What do I *hope* for in a guy? Everything . . .

Pause.

WAITRESS 1   What do I expect? Not much . . .

Pause.

filthy talk for troubled times

WAITRESS 1 What'll I *take?* Usually . . . anything . . .

MAN 3 *sits talking with* MAN 4 *and* MAN 1.

MAN 3 . . . no, I'm serious here. You ever see your parents doing it? That's an event you will never forget . . . believe you me. I mean, I never had any trouble walking in on my mother after she just got outta the shower—to be honest, when I was in, like, junior high . . . most weekdays, I'd skip home from football early so I could catch her toweling off—that's no problem. In fact, I'm of the opinion that it was actually healthy . . .

Pause.

MAN 3 But . . . I always had trouble with the idea of seeing my old man with his ass up in the air . . . I never could stomach that. Just didn't seem natural, you know? Here's my father, who was a dentist—and a good one, I hear—this is a man of responsibility . . . I never had a particular need to see this guy facedown in my mom's privates and cooing like a fucking baby. (*Beat.*) No thank you.

Pause.

MAN 3 One time, I was maybe twelve—Cub Scouts—I came in the house with my pinewood derby . . . The old man had worked like a beaver on that thing! Carving it, checking the weight, applying those little decals—first time I'd ever seen the guy touch a piece of fucking wood!—so, I get home, I'd just won a medal or some stupid-ass thing, I'm dying to show him . . . I run into their bedroom and . . . here he is with his dick down my mom's throat!

Pause.

MAN 3 Whoa! You can imagine my surprise at this seemingly unnatural coupling! I mean, this is a new one to me. I'm a kid, like I said, so it caught me off guard . . . but I was old enough to know that my mom's wisdom teeth weren't giving her any trouble and Dad probably had no good reason for having his wee-wee down her larynx . . .

Pause.

MAN 3   But I'm a model son, right? I'm not wanting to create a scene, so I stood and watched this spectacle for maybe . . . five minutes. Or so . . . I was transfixed! I mean, once my eyes adjusted to the dark.

Brief pause.

MAN 3   Damn. I just couldn't stand looking at his big ass . . . this dentist, my father . . . cramming his pe—his member—into my mom's face. It was kind of sad, actually . . .

Pause.

MAN 3   Then, just for a moment, a tiny shudder of ecstasy rolls through him and he pulls away . . . and . . . I'm staring into the face of Mrs. Freeman, our next-door neighbor. Ohh, fuck! She sees me, screams, I'm standing there pissing myself and stuttering . . . and you know what? That old shit just leans back on the comforter and says, between gasps, "How'd we do, son? Where's our trophy?"

Pause.

MAN 3   . . . I dove at him and crammed that fucking car in his ass right up to the cockpit. Like I said, I was a good kid, but everybody's got a breaking point, right? I snapped off one of the axles, but, by and large, I got most of that thing firmly in place . . .

Pause.

filthy talk for troubled times

MAN 3 Well . . . he never said a word about it . . . Mrs. Freeman pulled her skirt down and went back across the fence, my dad went into the bathroom to see what could be done to save the derby, and I just took off. Running. You know what? He never asked me to keep quiet about it. He never asked for my confidence or scolded me . . . never even complained of rectal discomfort, for that matter . . . although he did stand for dinner that night, come to think of it. Over at the kitchen counter.

Pause.

MAN 3 But: every week after that, on Mondays, and I mean without fail, I'd find a crisp new ten-dollar bill in my lunch box. Now try and fucking figure that one out! Yeah. The old man was complex, no doubt about that . . .

Pause.

MAN 3 So, fuck—it's been fifteen years, he and Mom are still together, the same house—I'm guessing this cash is gonna taper off, right? Everything's forgotten, as far as I'm concerned . . . but last week, I get a Western Union for a hundred and twenty bucks with a note. Says, "Sorry about the summer. We were vacationing in Canada. Love, Dad."

Pause.

MAN 3 It's a funny fucking world, isn't it?

MAN 5 *alone.*

MAN 5 . . . listen, you call it what you want, but it's a fucking *plague*, it really is. I mean, I can't even step in the Jacuzzi at my building anymore, it's that bad. Some guy, or some girl— where does it end, right?—up to their neck in those bubbles . . . How do I know if they've got some open sore or not? Is

that true or not? Right? You can't ask about something like
that without sounding personal. Believe me, I have tried.

Pause.

MAN 5   See, I'm taking no chances with this shit—you know my
neighborhood, no thank you. I turned away two Girl Scouts
selling *cookies* the other day, for chrissakes! Somebody
pinned a merit badge on them with an open cut . . . I'm on
machines next week coughing up blood. Nope, if I don't know
'em, they could be a carrier. Shit, two people I do know have
it! Haven't talked to them in weeks. All this research they're
doing, *nobody's* checked to see that it can't be transmitted
electronically. What do I know about the phone lines, right? I
say, put them all in a fucking pot and *boil* them . . . just as a
precaution.

Pause.

MAN 5   Still, I'm not totally callous . . . It's not like I don't drop
some change in those cans they have at the supermarket. I
want a cure as bad as the next person! It's just not fair, that's
all. I mean, who pays the price? I'm asking you . . . who pays
the . . . well, I guess they do *die* eventually, but that's not
really the point. It's you and me. Think about it. We date, we
try to fuck fairly respectable women . . . No, I mean it, I know
your type—all on the level, the usual set of positions—am I
right? I can tell these things . . . You don't do anything weird,
like, ahh, fruit? Do you? 'Cause I don't think the research
is in on stuff like that yet, so . . . be careful. Still, you're
normal! Very few drugs, you only dabble, same as me, no
transfusions—I mean, God, I have not used a pint of blood in
years . . . Basically, everything by the book.

Pause.

filthy talk for troubled times   47

MAN 5   *But* . . . who has to go around slipping paper under their thighs on the toilet seat? I won't even sit anymore—I just squat and hunch over—you know what I mean. Can't kiss your friends, shit, I'm bringing *canned* beverages out to dinner now! That is the fucking end! So, who pays the price? Right? I ask you. Jesus, those queer bastards!

Pause.

MAN 5   And all because someone wanted to get one up the ass or can't throw away a needle or, I dunno . . . grew up in fucking *Haiti* . . . (*Beat.*) You know what? Some people ruin it for everybody!

MAN 1 *talks with* MAN 3.

MAN 1   . . . what the fuck are you talking about? Hmm? Where do you get off calling me "insensitive"?

MAN 3   From listening to you! Don't you hear yourself? You're an insensitive bastard . . .

MAN 1   What?!

MAN 3   Fuck, wake up . . . face it. You're a prick, big deal . . .

MAN 1   Fine, and who the fuck are you?

MAN 3   I'm a piece of shit . . . but at least I recognize it.

Pause.

MAN 1   You're a crazy fuck. Insensitive? I'll tell you fucking *insensitive.* The other day, I'm in line at the supermarket—there's this guy in front of me with his hand full of change—and he's buying some fucking discount *vegetables*! Couple of eggplants, a mangy-looking carrot or two . . . but you know what? He's got a smile and "have a nice day" for the bitch at the register who is looking down her nose at him . . . That poor bastard is eating like a *refugee* and he's still got a sunny attitude! I tell you what, I nearly cried—I'm not fucking with ya, I nearly crawled on the floor and wept for this poor fuck, for all those poor, sad fucks like him . . . I was late for work so I couldn't stop and talk but it tore me up all the same. So next time, maybe you'd better just stop and *think* a minute before you start pointing your fucking finger, you son of a bitch!

Pause.

MAN 1 *moves off.* MAN 3 *looks after him.*

MAN 3   Shit . . . I wasn't implying that insensitivity was a *bad* thing! (*Beat.*) You dumb fuck . . .

MAN 4 *stands talking.*

MAN 4   . . . you know, one of these days I gotta stop fucking. I mean it . . .

Pause.

MAN 4   . . . I gotta get on with my life.

MAN 1 *sits at a table with* MAN 5.

MAN 1   Fuck . . . fuck it . . . I mean . . . Ahhhh, fuck . . .
MAN 5   Yeah.
MAN 1   Shit! Ohh . . . fuck. Fuck *that* . . . I'm just . . . ohh, fuck!
MAN 5   Hey, I'm here for you.
MAN 1   But . . . she . . . awwwwww, fuck this . . . This is . . . it's all fucked. I'm . . . Fuck, fuck! I mean, *fuck!*
MAN 5   Go on . . . get it out . . . go ahead.
MAN 1   . . . fuck . . .
MAN 5   Sure . . . that's it.

Pause.

MAN 1   You know? I mean . . . ahh . . . I really just . . . shit. I really needed her.

filthy talk for troubled times   49

Pause.

MAN 5 What? The fuck you talking about?

MAN 5 *looks at* MAN 1, *perplexed, and moves away.*

MAN 2 *stands alone.*

MAN 2 . . . me? Why am I smiling? Because I know. You know?
I mean, "I *know*." I'm aware of what's going on, okay? (*Beat.*)
I'm the quiet one, guy who doesn't say much, speak unless
spoken to. Nod my head and "yeah, yeah, yeah" all night, not
bat an eye, so be it. Easygoing. Like . . . some boy your sister
dated in high school. Harmless . . .

Pause.

MAN 2 And it doesn't matter what's going on—genocide,
an African village, a tractor-trailer jumps the median and
jackknifes on a school van . . . some gal has a bleeding spell,
it seeps all over my new Posturepedic—doesn't get me down.
I just keep smiling. (*Beat.*) Why? Because inside, I'm taking
it all in . . . and God, I'm laughing! I'm doubled over, tears
running down, I can't catch my breath I find it all so funny.
'Cause everywhere I look, far as the human cornea can make
out . . . all I see are niggers, and women, and old folks and
fucking foreign types. And all of 'em, scrambling around,
clawing each other just to get my crumbs! It's like a vision,
like some fucking revelation . . . them scattered around, like
worker ants, cowering at my feet, as I tower over 'em, chewing
down anything in my path.

Pause.

MAN 2 . . . so some black person elbows me, knocks me off my
bike in the park. Wave of the hand. Some cunt cuts in front,
checkout, "ten items," she's juggling *seventeen* . . . let it go.

(*Beat.*) See, I've got 'em in the long run. Because I'm a guy. And I'm white. And I've got a job. *And* I'm alive. That's right— I am their worst fucking nightmare and I'm not going anywhere and that, *that* just makes me howl with pleasure! 'Cause it's so perfect . . . and so dangerous.

Pause.

MAN 2   . . . some homeless dick, snot running down, hundred degrees, the subway . . . he's staring *me* down? Go for it, pal! Mixed-up fuck'll never realize that I eat dudes like him for breakfast, and later on? I just shit out *diamonds* . . . (*Beat.*) See, you can't do anything wrong when you're one of us.

Pause.

MAN 2   So, they can push and shove, gimme the finger or make eyes at me across the room. Doesn't matter a single bit. 'Cause they're lepers. They are, every last one of 'em . . . fucking freaks and monsters, and I can't get enough. I can't! I wanna hold 'em, I want to scoop them up in my arms and say, "Thank you! Thank you all for being so much less than me!" Seriously, they make me so very happy. (*Beat.*) And *that* is why I'm smiling, okay?

WAITRESS 2 *talks.*

WAITRESS 2   . . . so, I got the results back on Tuesday. I passed it with flying colors . . . Is that sweet? God, I was sure that guy I was with at Club Med had it—body like a god, beautiful—got him back to the room, we're in the shower . . . his fucking crotch is the color of *rhubarb*! I mean, nasty shit—and I still fucked him! Jesus, I need some serious therapy, ya know? But I passed the fucker . . . not a trace.

Pause.

WAITRESS 2 They found a lump—fucking clinic! It's not even their job. It was a "freebee," I guess. Little bastard is lodged right up under my boob. I probably should've caught it . . . but I could never get into all the self-check bullshit. Fuck that, I have guys fondling me night and day, you'd think someone would've had the courtesy to pass it along.

Pause.

WAITRESS 2 Oh, well . . . big fucking deal. Cut my tits off, see if I care! (*Beat.*) Least I'm not gonna die of some fucking STD. I'll still have my pride . . .

MAN 5 *alone.*

MAN 5 . . . and then, sometimes, I see myself as shit. No, I do. 'Cause I will be out there, times it hits me, at the pharmacy, the street, video store, maybe—snatching the last copy of a new release, out from under some handicapped lady. I could give two shits about it, just wanna see her eyes well up—and I'll be doing this and I nearly stop. Right? Stop and think to myself, "Christ, what the fuck am I doing? Huh?!" And I wanna go to her, turn her around in line there, and say, "Hey, listen, whatever it is that's wrong with you, I mean, whatever the fuck it is about your person that irritates me so fucking much . . . I don't care. I do not care. *It's okay.*" And I just give her the thing. Yeah, and we'd, I don't know, you know, stand there, I guess, or maybe go get a cup o' coffee—just let the world and all its worries pass us the fuck by.

Pause.

MAN 5 But then I think, "What good would that do?" So I don't. (*Beat.*) But I suffer because of it. Seriously . . . Things I say, guys I fuck over at work, the drop of a hat, or women. *All* those women. I reflect now and then about that stuff. Question it or study myself in the mirror. I'm always looking,

Neil LaBute

asking, "Who am I? Am I indeed this very shit that I imagine myself to be?"

Pause.

MAN 5   And the answer is always the same. "No." No, I'm not. I am just fucking *human*. This very *human* being. That's all. Not good, not bad . . . just me.

Lights slowly fade up to original tableau.

Brief tableau: The men stand or sit apart now, more alienated than before. The waitresses are cleaning up.

MAN 1   . . . all right, so you found her attractive . . .
MAN 2   . . . hey, nothing wrong with being conservative . . .
WAITRESS 2   . . . we could do away with men entirely . . .
MAN 5   . . . it's not like I'm dying to meet somebody . . .
MAN 3   . . . but if she invites me in . . .
MAN 4   . . . yeah, that's low-class . . .

MAN 2 *moves to* WAITRESS 1. *He whispers in her ear.*

WAITRESS 1   . . . no, I don't think so.

MAN 2 *starts to move off.*

MAN 2   Fuuuc . . .

He stops himself and turns to WAITRESS 1. *He smiles at her.*

MAN 2   . . . thanks anyway.

He returns to a corner as the men stare off, silent. The waitresses continue clearing up.

Silence. Darkness.

filthy talk for troubled times

the
new
testament

production history

The New Testament had its world premiere in August 2009 at the Open Fist Theatre Company in Los Angeles in a production directed by Bjorn Johnson.

characters

PRODUCER   white or black, fifties, can be cast as either a man
or a woman

WRITER   white, forties, a man

ACTOR   yellow, thirties, a man

setting

A restaurant near Chinatown.

time

Later this afternoon.

AUTHOR'S NOTE: If desired, the part of the "actor" can be played
by someone of a different race wearing yellowface for effect.
A slash in the dialogue denotes a suggested point of overlap
between that line and the next actor's line.

Silence. Darkness.

Three people sitting at a table—any configuration that you like, as long as they're seated. It is a restaurant, after all. Most people sit.

One guy is Asian (whichever kind you like—the ACTOR*), one guy is white (the* WRITER*), and the other person (man or woman—the* PRODUCER*) is probably white, too. Mix it up if you want to make it interesting.*

They sit, staring at one another for a moment. The PRODUCER *points at a dessert on the table.*

PRODUCER   . . . sure you don't wanna try it? / It's supposedly some kind of delicacy.

ACTOR   No thanks. / No thank you.

PRODUCER   *Sure*? It's made with a . . .

ACTOR   Yep. Totally sure. (*Beat.*) So?

PRODUCER   Ummmmmm . . . look . . . this is . . . I don't even know where to . . . (*To* WRITER.) Can you jump in here? Please?

WRITER   Sure, of course. (*To* ACTOR.) How ya doing?

ACTOR   Fine. *Was.*

WRITER   Yeah, I know . . . this is a bitch, a real *situation*, it is, but hey . . .

ACTOR   Of your making.

WRITER   True, right, yes . . . (*Toward dessert.*) I'm gonna just try this if that's okay. I love coconut.

ACTOR   Great.

PRODUCER   We should probably get down to the . . .

ACTOR   . . . I'm not sure what this is even . . .

WRITER   Hold on, I just want a quick . . .

ACTOR   Look. If this is gonna be some kind of . . .

WRITER   No, wait, I don't want you thinking . . . (*To* PRODUCER.) Ummm, God, that's good! Try it. Seriously. (*To* ACTOR.) It's a mistake, that's all. A misunderstanding that I'm trying to clear up. Right now, before we get too far into the . . . you know . . .

ACTOR   . . . "mistake"? / Me?

WRITER   Yeah. Essentially. / In this part, yes.

ACTOR   My being cast?

PRODUCER   Mmm. An *innocent* mistake. (*To* ACTOR.) Have a bite. It's like *twelve* calories. That's all mousse, it's not even cream-based.

ACTOR   No thanks.

WRITER   Really? That isn't cream? / Wow.

PRODUCER   Taste it. / See?

WRITER   No, you're right. It's lighter. Really fresh! (*To* ACTOR.) I wasn't in town. The casting—a lot of it, anyway—was done when I was over in Europe. I was at a one-act fest . . . I get a bunch of productions in, like, Germany and Poland . . . It doesn't matter, *places*. And so I was over there. Yeah. And then this whole thing happened and I got here, no sleep, and I realize what the director has done, and you know Vince, right? I mean, you've worked with . . . uh-huh. He's *different*. He likes to . . . what does he call it? "Challenge" people. To push the . . . not even the envelope, but the *perception* of the envelope, just, you know, like the *edge* of the envelope because believe me, he likes having a hit, too. We've had one together, him and me, and he was . . . well, it doesn't matter. Trust me, he liked it! So. There. (*Beat.*) Does that help?

PRODUCER   Ummmm . . . / Listen . . . can we just . . . ?

ACTOR   No. uh-uh. / Not at all.

Silence as the three parties look at one another. Waiting.

WRITER   Oh. (*To* PRODUCER.) I don't know what else to say. (*To* ACTOR.) "I'm sorry." How's that?

ACTOR   That doesn't really do shit, either.

WRITER   No, I didn't think it would, but at least I said it, which is, I dunno. Something. This line of work.

PRODUCER   I think what he means is: we're really so sorry about this. *Very.* (*To* WRITER.) True?

WRITER   Yeah. (*Beat.*) I mean, it's not really our fault—yours or mine—because Vince does not listen, he's like a schoolboy at some picnic, running around with a . . . but yeah. I'm sorry it got to this place. Obviously I am. (*Beat.*) We're all human here.

PRODUCER   We are. / That's a good point. To keep it on those terms—the "human factor."

ACTOR   But . . . / No, see, that's not . . . no. Sorry.

PRODUCER   What?

ACTOR   That doesn't do me any good here. Okay? You guys being sorry—I *want* this part. / You gave it to me already!
(*To* PRODUCER.) *You* were in the room.

PRODUCER   I know, but . . . / I *know* that. I agree.

WRITER   Yeah, thanks for that. Really helps the cause here . . .

PRODUCER   He's right, though . . . I agreed with the casting, but it is Vince's production . . .

WRITER   . . . of *my* play! You know that! We've had this conversation a thousand times. It's his *version* of my work. The work is *mine.* My contract guarantees me "meaningful dialogue" in matters of casting. So . . . (*To* ACTOR.) And I'm sorry, but there's no way—that is, none, as in impossible— you should've been cast in that role! I am sorry.

PRODUCER   Very sorry. Really. / Oh, God . . . let's . . .

ACTOR   No. / No, I don't accept that.

WRITER   Well, now you're just being difficult. Or what's that other word? That people use when some Asian person is . . . inscrutable? Yes. / That's it. And you are being. That. You're "inscrutable."

ACTOR   What? / You did not just say that . . .

WRITER   Hey, you're the one doing it! I'm just pointing it out. (*Takes another bite.*) This stuff really is magnificent. (*To* ACTOR.) I can't believe you're from over there—the Far East or wherever—and you don't like coconut. (*Beat.*) That's weird.

ACTOR   I live in Seattle!

WRITER   Sure. *Now.* But I mean . . . you know . . .

PRODUCER   Maybe we should get back to the subject at hand. All right? (*Beat.*) Listen . . .

WRITER   Fine. I was just making conversation . . .

ACTOR   You're an idiot. Both of you.

the new testament   61

He stands, grabs at his jacket on the back of the chair.

ACTOR   I don't have to sit here and listen to . . . "coconut"?! I mean, what the fuck?!

WRITER   . . . hey, nice mouth . . .

ACTOR   I'll go to Equity. / I'll see my lawyer, or some—we can let them sort it out.

PRODUCER   Whoa, hold on there . . . / Come on, now!

WRITER   Why do you have to say crap like that? We are reaching out here. *Talking.*

ACTOR   As you make slurs about my . . . about *me* . . .

WRITER   When? What'd I say, that your people came from the Far East? Am I *way* off the mark on that one? Huh? I don't think so. Look, you're not *French*, let's face it . . . and who wants to be, anyway, in this day and age? Being French is way past cool. / I've got some French in me and I hardly tell anybody . . .

ACTOR   This is ridiculous. / To stand here and . . .

WRITER   So, sit then. Sit and let's talk.

PRODUCER   Please do. *Please.*

The ACTOR looks around, makes a decision. Sits on the end of his seat.

ACTOR   Five minutes. That's what I'll give you. / And Chinatown? Why the hell are we . . . Did you do this for *me*?

PRODUCER   Thank you. Thanks. We appreciate it. / No! God no—it's just a restaurant. (*Beat.*) Now listen, we're very, very . . .

WRITER   Hey, don't speak for me. (*To* ACTOR.) I'm happy to talk about this but let's not get all . . . you know, *weepy* here. Please. I'm as much the injured party as you, I don't care what you think.

PRODUCER   . . . can we not get into the . . . ?

ACTOR   Excuse me? (*To* WRITER.) You're *what*?

WRITER   Actors come and go, pal—you guys are the *furniture*, okay? What I write is the *house*. Let's not get all precious about it . . .

ACTOR I can't believe the shit that comes out of your mouth . . .
I mean, for being a . . .

WRITER Yeah? Well, maybe you should come out of the *gym*
once a week and take a look at the world around you. Okay?

ACTOR What does that mean?

WRITER It means—and I'm not alone in this—you're not the
most beloved species on the planet, my friend. / The "act-or."

ACTOR Oh really? / (*To* PRODUCER.) Is that right?

PRODUCER Well . . . we try not to be too . . . but it's . . .
Gentlemen, this really isn't getting us anywhere, so can we
just . . .

WRITER Pretty much. And *I* need you guys! Ask the common
person who goes to the movies or buys HBO or maybe goes
to see a play, like, oh, maybe every eight *months* . . . They
think you're a bunch of overpaid jackasses who can't keep it
in your pants for more than six minutes at a time. You don't
like what's happened here? Huh? Go cry on a sack of *money.*
Most people work for a living . . .

The ACTOR *looks back and forth at the defiant* WRITER *and the
sheepish* PRODUCER. *Stands.*

ACTOR Amazing how fast five minutes goes . . . (*To* PRODUCER.)
I'll see you in court.

WRITER Not before I see you doing *The Mikado.*

The ACTOR *starts to lunge at the* WRITER, *and the* PRODUCER *jumps
to his/her feet, blocking him.*

PRODUCER Stop it! Both of you!

Before the ACTOR *can get away the* PRODUCER *wraps an arm
around his shoulder. Holding him tight.*

ACTOR Please let go of me . . . / Stop it!

PRODUCER Come on, now, please . . . / Let me just lay out the
offer we were going to . . .

WRITER   Let him go . . . For God's sake, you're just embarrassing
everybody with your . . .

PRODUCER   Stay out of this for a minute! (*To* ACTOR.) We have an
offer for you. A real offer of substance—can't you please just
hear it out? *Please?*

WRITER   The guy's a hothead . . . It's like dealing with North
Korea. I mean . . .

The PRODUCER *holds onto the* ACTOR *for dear life—after a moment,
he calms down and listens. Still breathing hard.*

ACTOR   I'll speak with *you* . . . (*To* WRITER.) Not to him.

WRITER   Oh, sure, the one with the money you'll listen to. That
sounds about right.

PRODUCER   Just eat the dessert for a second, okay?! Can you
just . . . ?

The WRITER *is about to say something else but lets it go. Takes
another bite of dessert.*

WRITER   This thing really is amazing—there's a layer of lemon
zest or something in it, and then . . . I dunno, I'd say "cake"
but that's not right . . . it's almost like a flaky . . .

The others look over at him—waiting for him to finish.

WRITER   *What?* It's good, I can't help it. I'm an artist—I
appreciate art. (*To* PRODUCER.) Go ahead, say what you were
saying . . .

PRODUCER   All right, listen—obviously this is a very delicate
situation and we're not trying to offend you here, or the
community at large or whatever. / Your *race.* Anyone.

ACTOR   Fine. / *All right,* and?

PRODUCER   *And* . . . we are willing to offer you another part in the
company. Of equal value if at all possible . . . or we might be
willing . . .

ACTOR   How are you gonna do that? Huh?

PRODUCER Well . . .

WRITER Hey, there's some good roles in there . . .

ACTOR Yeah, but . . . that's not . . .

PRODUCER Right, and we feel that you might be . . . a man of your talents and, and . . . of your many *qualities* might be excellent as . . .

ACTOR You cast me as Jesus! *Jesus!* What part is gonna be equal to that? / Tell me . . .

The WRITER *and the* PRODUCER *nod at each other—they are trying to think on their feet but it's not happening.*

PRODUCER Yes, that's true, but . . . / Well, there's many . . . *Judas* is good . . . or, ummmm . . .

ACTOR Oh, I see! I had the lead, but now you'll let me play the bad guy! / No, I get it . . .

PRODUCER That's not the . . . / He isn't *so* bad . . .

ACTOR He *betrays* Christ! He's the villain!

WRITER Yeah, and?

ACTOR So, it's okay for the Asian guy to play that, to be all . . . but not Jesus! Right?

WRITER No, that's not . . . You're being a bit simplistic. / It's a revisionist piece, anyway, and Judas has a number of real insights throughout that are . . . Didn't you ever see *Jesus Christ Superstar*? Black dude stole the show—plus, in this one he's got all the laughs! Seriously, *all.*

ACTOR Oh *really* . . . / I don't care! *I'm* Jesus!

WRITER But we didn't cast you! I mean, *I* didn't and that's all that matters to me. (*Beat.*) I'm sorry, but you can't play the son of God. Nope. Can't. Is not gonna happen . . .

ACTOR And why not? (*Beat.*) Go on, tell me . . . I'd like to hear you say it. (*Beat.*) Why not?

WRITER Ummm . . . I'm sorry, I didn't bring my copy of *The Last Supper* with me today, I was traveling light, but if you'd care to go upstairs into any room—that's any, of the, say, ohh, three hundred plus rooms here at the Hilton—you will find a nice little Bible waiting for you in the chest of drawers. Crack it open, glance at any of the many pictures inside of Jesus. The Savior. Of *all* mankind, buddy. Even you and your bunch—he's not a Chinaman. Okay? I don't wanna get into a pissing contest with you or anything, but he's not. He's not a black man, he's not a lady, and he isn't some alien from Mars. It's just a cold, hard fact and you can lash out . . . do your little dance and point fingers, blame whoever you want for being born who you are but the fact remains: he looked like this. (*Points to own face.*) Like me. He did and that's just the way it goes. (*Beat.*) I mean, God, you're making this *so* demeaning and ugly and if the shoe was on the other . . . you would not cast me to act in a show about . . . well, whoever. Buddha or somebody like that. Was he a god for you guys? I don't even know now, I'm so worked up about this—I believe he was. Or some kinda religious deal. The Dalai Lama. I'm not sure which type you are. Korean? I don't know and that doesn't immediately make me a racist. It doesn't. I didn't see your resume so I'm just out here guessing—I knew a Korean girl in college that I got very close to and you have a similar look to hers. The bigger forehead thing and a bit of a—anyway—that's all I've got to say. There. (*Beat.*) It's, like, imagine Brad Pitt in *Raisin in the Sun*! Crazy, right? You'd never do something as stupid as that, would you? / Right?

ACTOR That's not even . . . / . . . the same . . .

PRODUCER God, I'd produce that in a second! I mean if he'd do it. That'd sell like a . . .

WRITER Not. Helping. (*To* PRODUCER.) Shhhh!

PRODUCER Sorry . . . so. / (*To* ACTOR.) I am prepared to make an offer. To you. Right now.

ACTOR Oh-my-God . . . / You did not just say all that shit to me. I am going to pretend that I fell asleep and, and . . . I had a really disturbing dream that is about to be over. *Is* over, right now, because . . .

WRITER So, go on then, get all smart about it—can you deny what I'm saying? Huh? Jesus was not some . . . Indonesian guy! He just wasn't.

ACTOR I'm not *Indonesian*! Jesus Christ!

WRITER Exactly! That's his name—"Jesus *Christ*." Not "Jesus Fujihama-Kurosawa*!*" Sorry.

ACTOR You are such a fucking . . . *moron* . . .

WRITER . . . and *now* the name-calling starts . . .

PRODUCER Guys, can we please just . . . please!

ACTOR How can you write such beautiful stuff? Hmm? How?!

WRITER It's called "talent," okay? I mean . . .

ACTOR But such lovely language and ideas and, and . . . you're this . . . no, no, no! It's not right! / It's impossible!

WRITER Oh, *please*. / I say *one* thing about you as a person—I didn't make you Asian, it's not my fault—and you gotta go straight at my work and my, my, whatever! Saying shit about my ability to, to, to . . .

ACTOR This can't be happening!

PRODUCER Let me just lay out the proposal that we have for you here . . . / But it's very . . .

ACTOR No! *No!* / And why shouldn't I be able to play Jesus, anyway? Why not? Color-blind casting is a regular part of the American theater—it's practically passé!

WRITER That's right! It is, and I don't want to be *passé*! Okay? Do you mind? It's *my* show!

ACTOR That's just ignorant. You're a foolish . . .

WRITER Says you. An out-of-work Asian guy. (*To* PRODUCER.) Can't we just throw some money at this guy and make him go away? Sandy?

The PRODUCER *shakes his/her head—the* WRITER *throws his hands up in the air.*

ACTOR No. You can't. (*Beat.*) I have a contract.

WRITER Lucky you. Only thing keeping me from asking you outside to settle this.

ACTOR Go ahead. I'm a black belt, shithead.

WRITER Wow. What a surprise . . . an Asian who knows *karate*.

ACTOR Oh-my-God! Is *everything* that comes out of your mouth offensive?!

WRITER About seventy percent.

the new testament   67

PRODUCER . . . that might be a little low . . . (*Gets a look from* WRITER.) Come on, Steve, I'm not saying anything new here. You're a bit of a . . . (*Beat.*) What?! I'm just *mentioning* . . .

The WRITER *throws the* PRODUCER *another look—"whose side are you on?"*

WRITER Whatever! (*Beat.*) Listen, bud . . . I don't give two shits about color-blind casting or what's fair or any of that crap. I did not put your family in an internment camp or come up with the idea of slavery or . . . who knows what? What's the South African thing that I always mix up with "apathy"? (*Thinks.*) "Apartheid!" That wasn't me, so just get down off your high horse, okay?

PRODUCER Look, let me just lay out our *plan* so I can . . . I want us to remain friendly here! Even *if* money is exchanged, we'd like to, you know, still be . . .

WRITER Why do we have to buy this guy off? Huh? Why can't we just say what we feel to a person without having to pay for it? It's such a crock of . . . It's *wrong,* that's what it is. (*To* PRODUCER.) It's blackmail, pure and simple, let's at least call it by its real name. "Blackmail."

PRODUCER No, now let's not get all . . . No one's said anything about . . .

ACTOR It's not blackmail!—I'm simply fighting for what's right here! Not my dignity or the idea of, you know, the theater as a place where the imagination can run and be free . . . not for any of that . . . this is a simple case of right and wrong!

WRITER . . . I have a meeting at one, so can you get to the point?

ACTOR The point is this! Here is the goddamn *point*—I was hired, by a director who is directing this play, interpreting it in his own way and being paid by you, the producer of said show, to do just that. (*Beat.*) Now, I may be a quirky choice, I might be, that's true, I might be . . . a *surprising* choice, who knows, but maybe I'm an inspired choice, that's what I think—when he cast me I didn't get all excited just because I booked the *job*, I was thrilled that someone today was willing to take a chance like this. To put a foot down against tired old values and a stock way of seeing things. (*Beat.*) I want to play "Jesus" because Jesus is love and anybody should be able to play that. Any person on earth is supposed to be able to reach to those heights, and so why not me? Hmmmm? Why shouldn't I, in this day and age, how come it shouldn't be someone of my background out there as much as anyone else? This is what we need. The world, I mean. (*To* WRITER.) Your words are so beautiful in this thing . . . you show *such* understanding and warmth . . . Why can't you see this? Why don't you realize how much good could come from our production as it puts its hands out to the audience and says: "This is the face of Jesus today. *This* is the true power of God. Without color. Without judgment . . . " (ACTOR *gets a little teary now.*) I'm sorry, but this obviously means a great deal to me.

The WRITER *and the* PRODUCER *sit, looking at him. Silence as the words of the* ACTOR *wash over them for a moment.*

PRODUCER   Well . . . that was really impassioned, thank you for that, Lee. / No, I mean it.

ACTOR   It's how I feel. / Can't help it . . .

WRITER   Are you gay?

ACTOR   Excuse me?

WRITER   No, I'm just curious—the way you went on and on there, it just made me wonder. Are you?

ACTOR   You can't ask me that.

WRITER   Since when is that a secret? Most gays I know have practically tattooed *rainbows* on their asses, they're *sooo* excited to tell you about their . . . you know . . . all that faggy stuff about 'em. This and that and their favorite *designers* . . . and . . .

ACTOR   So?

WRITER   And now I ask you and you don't wanna say anything about it?

the new testament   69

ACTOR Look, an actor's sexuality shouldn't have anything to do with playing a part, or . . .

WRITER I didn't say it did. I just asked you a question . . . Do-you-like-guys?

PRODUCER Gentlemen, this might not be the time . . .

WRITER . . . are you gonna finish that dessert?

ACTOR Then when is? Huh?! When are you supposed to confront ignorance and prejudice and, and . . . blind intolerance?! You tell me . . . you're the one with all the Tonys, so why don't you tell me when? (*To* PRODUCER.) You've got a chance to do the right thing here—to continue doing what you already felt in your heart, but you have to be a little bit brave, just this much—(*shows this with his fingers*)—come on, Sandy, it's not so far to go, to do a good and honest thing, just a little further! If you do, *so* many people will applaud you and get behind all of your work, not just this play but everything you do. / They honestly will . . .

PRODUCER But . . . / You need to understand the fine print of my . . . the *complications* of . . . It is not a simple case of me being able to do anything I want. (*To* ACTOR.) If it was just *me* then there might be a . . .

ACTOR Please! I'm begging you now, not just for me but for everyone, people of all faiths and creeds and colors . . . *all* of us . . .

WRITER Hey, Bruce Lee, just so you know? Creeds and faiths are pretty much the same deal. Not exactly, but almost, so . . .

ACTOR I'm not talking to you right now!

WRITER Yeah, but you shouldn't make yourself look stupid if you can help it . . .

ACTOR Fine! You know what I'm saying! (*Back to* PRODUCER.) People will accept this, if we play it with the proper sensitivity . . . the correct amount of gravitas that any play of this nature deserves. They know we're not just fucking around here—they can see we're doing something really new and special and that all our hearts—*most* of them, anyway—are in the right place. It could really be something momentous, a rare thing.

Neil LaBute

WRITER   Yeah?

ACTOR   *Yes!* I feel it. In my very bones . . . and in my soul. That deep inside me.

WRITER   Right, but no offense, you guys eat dogs for lunch and many of us in the West here find that disgusting, so . . .

ACTOR   I'm not *Korean*, you prick! I'm of Chinese descent but I was born in Idaho! I-da-ho. You got that? / My God . . .

WRITER   Huh. / Interesting . . .

PRODUCER   All right, look, can we all just decide to take a step back here and see if we can find some common ground? Please?

WRITER   I like egg drop soup—does that count?

ACTOR   You're a fucking dick, you know that?

WRITER   Kinda.

PRODUCER   Listen, guys, this isn't helping us—we have to find a way to . . .

WRITER   Okay, fine. (*Turns to* ACTOR.) How you feel about *Othello*?

PRODUCER   Steve, can we just . . . ? (*Beat.*) You *always* bring this up when we get into a conversation about . . . / It doesn't matter . . .

WRITER   No, hold on . . . / It's a legitimate thing I'm asking here! In light of all the rest of what's going down. (*To* ACTOR.) So? How do you feel about white guys playing that part?

ACTOR   Ummm, I dunno. It's complicated. It's a beautiful play. I do love Shakespeare—I got the chance to play "Prince Hal" for Anne Bogart at Columbia when I was a senior.

WRITER   . . . figures. (*To himself.*) A *chick.*

ACTOR   Excuse me?

WRITER   Nothing. Go ahead.

ACTOR   It was amazing. Great production.

WRITER   So, you were "Hal," *English* prince who becomes the King of *England.* That "Hal"?

ACTOR   Yes. That one. (*Beat.*) Any problems with that?

PRODUCER   Guys, let's . . . just . . .

ACTOR   No, he asked me. I want to hear what he has to say. (*To* WRITER.) Go on.

WRITER   It's fine. It's whatever you want, that's the beauty of

the new testament   71

theater, right? It's all a big illusion, so I guess that just makes it open season for people like you to . . . play your kinda parts and then whatever else you feel like grabbing from . . .

ACTOR What does that mean? "People like me"?

WRITER It's all fake! We know it is, so it's no big deal if you wanna add insult to, you know, injury . . . go play the king or, or the "queen," for that matter, because . . .

ACTOR I'm not gay! / Stupid bastard . . .

PRODUCER This isn't helping! / Can we stop now?!

WRITER I didn't mean that! I'm saying if it was a movie it'd be different—which is kind of odd, when you think about it, they're just pictures run past our eyes so fast that it seems real but it's not—but we demand a certain kind of *truth* there. If ol' Anne whatever-her-name-is was making a film she couldn't get away with that shit, *that's* what I'm saying . . . (*Beat.*) But it's just a play, it's all just make-believe, anyway, right? So let's go get bombed out of our skulls in the lobby bar and "pretend" that all this is possible—theater is just so full of shit now it's almost entirely lost its ability to, to connect with people . . . its audience. And stuff like this—I'm sorry but an Asian "Jesus"—it is just paving the way for folks to turn and walk the other way. To say "forget this crap, it's bullshit . . . " (*To* PRODUCER.) So, do what you want. You love the idea so damn much, I'm not gonna stand in your way. I'm just the guy who was pacing in the wings pointing out how fucking absurd the idea is. A yellow Jesus! I mean, please! Just . . . *please.* Okay? You guys do it and be cutting-edge and so cool and all that, but just remember this conversation and that one guy—*me*—one of us had the balls to shake his head and be that voice of reason. The unpopular one . . . the *fascist* who actually has a point when everybody stops screaming in his face and takes a look around—I'll be the one who is standing there shrugging his shoulders and saying "I told ya so" when we close out-of-town. When the only place you can sell a ticket is *Guam*, I'll be *that* guy reminding you that the gods were looking down and they did not approve. (*To* ACTOR.)

Neil LaBute

You are not "Jesus," I'm sorry, dude, but it's true. Facts are
facts.

ACTOR You just don't get it . . . you're so . . .

WRITER No, *you* don't! You're stubborn and you've got an ego the
size of . . . Mongolia. (*Beat.*) Sorry. That was uncalled for. You
are one talented guy, I get that—I enjoy you on your show, I
watch it regularly—and you can be a lot of different people,
true, transform your persona into a variety of folks, but not
Jesus. Not the son of God and redeemer of all mankind. It
just doesn't matter how you twist or turn it, you cannot be
him. I'm sorry, but you just can't . . .

The men stop now, staring at each other. Quiet descends.

WRITER A line has to be drawn somewhere and this is right about
where I draw it—somewhere out there is an audience who
wants to see Genghis Khan play Henry V, then okay, that is
cool by me, but I'm the guy who wrote *this* play and I get a say.
I get to step up and put my foot down and the time for that is
now. The Jesus in my play is one of those . . . you know . . .
he's a *white* dude! And don't do the whole "look where he's
from . . . probably looked like Cat Stevens" game with me,
either. Don't-give-a-shit. In my world, he's white. Blue eyes and
some . . . longish hair. He's cute, but not too cute. Not *girly* . . .
(*Beat.*) *That's* what I'm trying to say to you here, Lee, and it's
not anything for you to take offense at: that guy is not *you*.
It's so simple, really, and unless you're up for playing him in
whiteface, then I'm of the mind-set that you should take the
very generous offer of our fine producer here and back out of
the party with as much grace and "by your leave" as you can
muster. All right? Enjoy your hiatus . . . (*Beat.*) Can we sign
something now and get this going or what?

Silence. The ACTOR *looks at both of the other people and then puts
out a hand. Snaps his fingers.*

ACTOR   Fine! Let me see it, then . . . come on.

The PRODUCER *sits up and gropes around in his/her pocket; he/
she pulls out an envelope. Removes a document from it and
hands it over to the* ACTOR, *who scans it.*

WRITER   Nice, huh? Healthy little *donation* to your retirement fund
    there . . .
ACTOR   It is. Very nice. (*Beat.*) Wow.
PRODUCER   We're trying to show you some respect. I know it
    seems like we're . . . but we are.
ACTOR   No, I can see that, it's . . . My goodness.
WRITER   We should've done this in the beginning. Right from the
    . . . you know? (*To* PRODUCER.) This is how shit gets done. With
    cash.
ACTOR   . . . right . . . okay, I'm . . . huh.
PRODUCER   And I'm happy to speak with my colleagues about
    you for my next show . . . We're doing a revival starting in San
    Diego around this time next year, so . . .
ACTOR   Really? What is it?
PRODUCER   Oh, it's, ahhh . . . a musical.
ACTOR   Yeah? Which?
PRODUCER   *Flower Drum Song.* / But that's not the reason that
    I'm . . . / I wasn't implying . . .
ACTOR   Oh. / Uh-huh. / Yeah. *Sure.*

The ACTOR *shakes his head, mumbles something to himself, then
turns to the* PRODUCER *and* WRITER. *Smiles.*

ACTOR   . . . all right. / Okay, I'll do it.
WRITER   What? / You will? For sure, without all the . . .
ACTOR   Absolutely. Without question.
WRITER   Perfect!
PRODUCER   Oh, great. Whew! What a relief . . .
WRITER   Shake on it? / (*To* ACTOR.) Come on, a handshake is
    everything where I grew up. It's *totally* binding . . .
ACTOR   Ummmm . . . / Sure . . . of course. Why not?

The two men shake hands wholeheartedly. The PRODUCER *is quick to grab back the document and smooths it out. A pen appears magically in his/her hand.*

PRODUCER   This is really . . . if you'll just sign on the two lines there, we can get the . . .

ACTOR   No need.

PRODUCER   Excuse me?

WRITER   No, you gotta sign. That's part of the whole . . . thing. For us. You have to sign.

ACTOR   Why?

WRITER   Because you're . . . we need to have a . . .

ACTOR   I already agreed to do it.

WRITER   Yeah, exactly! So you have to . . .

ACTOR   No, I'm sorry. You didn't understand—I'm agreeing to play the part. Jesus. / In makeup. *White* makeup.

WRITER   . . . *what?* / Are you . . . ? No, no, no, no . . .

ACTOR   Should be very interesting. / *Very.*

WRITER   *What? No!* / You're not serious!

ACTOR   Deadly.

WRITER   But . . . but! (*To the* PRODUCER.) He can't do that! He can't just . . .

ACTOR   Can and did. / It was *your* idea, so thank you . . .

WRITER   No, it's . . . / Yeah, but I didn't . . . shit!

ACTOR   You shook on it, which is *binding.* Says you.

WRITER   Yeah, but I didn't mean . . . (*To* PRODUCER.) Help me out here!

PRODUCER   You did say it to him, Steve, I mean, you know . . . *technically* . . .

WRITER   So what?! It's his word against ours . . . / Come on . . .

PRODUCER   Oh. / So now you want me to lie about it?

WRITER   Fuck yes! Of course!

PRODUCER   No, that's not how I . . . That would be . . .

ACTOR   . . . I don't think you want to do that . . .

PRODUCER   . . . that is not something that I'm . . .

WRITER That's what producers do, lie! You're a born liar, just like the rest of us! We lie on paper, actors lie onstage, and you . . . you people lie to everybody else! *That's* the way it works!

PRODUCER Not for me it isn't. (*Beat.*) Sorry, no . . .

WRITER Yeah, well, then fuck you! You hear me? Hmmm? *Fuck you!*

PRODUCER No, Steve, I'm . . . You seem to be the one who just got fucked. You and you alone.

ACTOR Well put, Sandy . . .

WRITER Shut the hell up, asshole! Just shut up! (*Beat.*) Get that Pearl Harbor, didn't-I-just-pull-a-fast-one grin off your fucking face and listen to me! (*Points.*) I don't care what this motherfucker says, I will fight you to the goddamn Supreme Court if I have to! I mean, are you kidding me? Huh? Are you *fucking* kidding me? No way is there gonna be some slanty-eyed Jesus in my play and that's that! That is how it will *never* be, you got me?! Maybe in some Off-Broadway bullshit show you do or, or out there in the real world—maybe Christ himself'll come down from on high and prove me wrong, riding a golden *rickshaw* and laughing in my face—but not in one of my shows! *I* am God here, *me*, I am the creator and what I say goes and I say never! Never, never, not ever! *Never!*

The ACTOR *calmly stands and pulls on his coat. Looking at the* WRITER.

ACTOR You're absolutely right—it will not be that way because I, as promised to you, will be wearing *whiteface*. And contact lenses—do you prefer blue or green? (*To* PRODUCER.) He said "blue" earlier, didn't he?

PRODUCER . . . I believe so . . .

ACTOR So I'll need those . . . and not the scary Lil' Kim kind, okay? I'd rather have the more expensive ones that look real, so I would get hopping on that . . . and then the hair. Longish, right? (*Pointing.*) He said "longish" hair, for the part, wasn't that it? Cute but not too cute . . . not girlish. I think I'll just keep growing my own, so let's see if we can make that work . . . and the rest will just sorta find a way into the process.

That's how I usually do it, so let's just go from there. (*To* WRITER.) And you . . . *you* should open an atlas sometime. Take a look. The Middle East? It's in *Asia*. Yeah. Christ was *Asian*. (*Smiles.*) We good? Great. Thanks for the chat—see you at rehearsals. (*Holding up his fist.*) Peace.

The ACTOR *hesitates another moment, then turns and leaves slowly. Singing "I Enjoy Being a Girl."*

Long silence. The PRODUCER *turns to say something to the* WRITER, *who quickly holds up a hand.*

WRITER   . . . ah-ah-ah. Not a word. Not *one* word.

The PRODUCER *stops, turns away. The* WRITER *stares out. After a moment, without looking over, the* PRODUCER *says:*

PRODUCER   Coconut? (*Offers up the plate.*)

The WRITER *turns slowly to his* PRODUCER, *eyes blinking as he tries to stop himself from speaking. Just manages it.*

Without warning, the WRITER *turns the dessert over on the table. Splat! The cream (or whatever the hell it is) goes everywhere. He wipes at a bit of mess on his jacket, then stands up.*

WRITER   . . . "coconut" is a word.

The WRITER *turns and walks off. The* PRODUCER *watches him go.*

He/she reaches over and picks up some dessert with one finger. Touches it to his/her tongue. Waits.

Silence. Darkness.

i
love
this
game

production history

I Love This Game had its world premiere in June 2007 at the Mile Square Theatre in New Jersey in a production directed by Frank Licato.

characters

MAN   early forties

setting

Out near the ball field.

time

Day after day.

AUTHOR'S NOTE: The effect of the setting here should be almost dreamlike, a reality covered over by fog or mist. Maybe a streak of brightness from the stadium lights overhead.

Silence. Darkness.

A MAN *standing near the edge of the stage—he is dressed in casual clothes (sporting jersey, sweats, running shoes). He wears a baseball cap.*

MAN . . . I love this game. I do. That's one thing you should know about me, before we get all . . . I do love the game. Baseball. (*Beat.*) I mean, look, I've always followed my team, year in and out, I'm totally out there rooting for these guys whether it's on the field or me sitting in some crappy hotel bar—I used to travel a lot—but I'm not some fair-weather fan. Absolutely not, no. I'm with these guys year round, all hundred and . . . however many games in a season. If they make it to the playoffs, Series even, or they're sitting in the basement . . . I'm right there. (*Beat.*) I've even been down to spring training a couple times, so, ya know, I'm . . . yeah. This sport is my main thing. Absolutely. Not that I don't get into football or other crap like that, some hockey, whatever, but baseball is my game of choice, no question. *Without* question. I'm a baseball guy, that's me. It is.

He waits a moment, letting this sink in. He wipes at his brow.

MAN I'm also—not to, like, blow my own trumpet here or whatnot, but—I also coached a little, I did. Yep. I don't mean, you know, not in a *professional* capacity or anything, at college, no, but for these kids down at the . . . you know, whaddayacallit? The Parks and Rec Department. In the summer. I've been a batting coach with one of the teams there since my oldest—Dale, Jr.—he went and tried out one spring. Kid's a fantastic ballplayer, really is, walked on and took over the shortstop position from a neighbor boy who'd been on the squad for, like, *three* years previous, so . . . (*Beat.*) And he can hit, too. Unbelievable power for a young guy and this really great respect for the game. The rules and

i love this game

all that, you know? A regular little sportsman of the year, and I wanted to be a part of that, so I started helping kids learn to bat at some of the practices—holding the thing correctly, learning to swing through the pitch, finding their stance, etcetera. No big deal, really, but it can make a bit of a difference in somebody's career if a person like me takes an interest in them early on. Helps instill the *basics* at the right age . . . You'd be surprised. Lot of boys I've worked with have gone right on up through their school programs and been highly successful, including a few scholarships to various colleges, local anyway, and even one kid—played just after my son did—he's on this minor league team in the Seattle area, could even end up with a major league franchise if he plays his cards right. Guy's a home run hitter, long ball expert, but he also whiffs a lot, so, you know . . . we'll just see where that leads. Still, he's one of my boys and so I watch him on TV occasionally—you gotta have a satellite to even find his games—but I've seen him play and you know what? Still holds the bat *exactly* the way I showed him, maybe twelve years ago. Yep. (*Smiles.*) That's pretty damn satisfying. My kid, as good as he was, ended up working construction and only plays on weekends in the summer, so, you know—you gotta live the fantasy out through somebody else once in a while. Right? But my Dale knows I love 'im, no matter what he became, so, yeah, still plays a hell of an infield game, even if it's just slow pitch over there at the public fields. I go see him play some evenings, last game of the night on a Saturday and it just . . . well, you know how it is when it's your own son. It's just . . . pleasing.

The MAN *wipes at his brow again. Smiles.*

MAN   So lemme ask you . . . why're you looking at me like that? Huh? I'm thinking that . . . you probably recognize me, right? Realize that I'm somebody you know from somewhere but you can't put your finger on it yet. Isn't that it? Uh-huh. Tell ya what, I'll give you a hint and you'll probably get it right away. Just like that. (*Snaps fingers.*) Two years ago, Morgan Field. Cubs versus the Bobcats. You got it yet? No? I was the guy. You know . . . the *guy*, with the whole . . . It was on the news for, like, a month. The fight. The parents who, and we all got into a tussle and, you know, yeah. That was *me*. (*Beat.*) Yep, now you remember, don't ya? Sure. It was a big deal around here . . . even made the national news for a couple days there. Our pictures. And still, to this day, I do not get how it happened, I really don't . . . I said one thing—one!—this tiny comment about the way this guy's kid was crouching in the batter's box and, yes, okay, I made a bit of a joke out of the thing, I mean, you probably never saw any of the amateur video from that day but . . . it's still available out there, folks on the Internet and whatnot . . . but the kid did look pretty goofy. He was a terrible hitter from what I could see, this was, like, his fourth time at bat, and so I just yelled it out, no big deal; that's half of the Little League experience, dealing with the crowd. My kid did it, and he was an amazing player, but people would always be saying stuff, crazy stuff, about his name and his, I dunno, his *socks* and shit, the point was to try and throw the kids off! That's the *idea* behind it . . . and this guy goes ballistic in the crowd. From the visitor bleachers way over on the opposite side of the field he comes running over, running straight at me . . . I can see what he's doing, and he looks like he's, you know, like he's out of his head, swearing and almost crying he's so red in the face and these, like, beads of water (I don't know if they're tears or what) coming off him. A couple dads down front try to stop him, but he plows right through them—knocks over a mom holding her baby, even!—and he hits me like a train coming out of a tunnel. Up over the stands and down onto the metal seats, him swinging these wild punches as I'm defending myself and screaming up into his face. Choking and hissing at him, with these people gathering behind him and grabbing his neck, but he's . . . he's not going anywhere, won't give up . . . He's sitting on my chest, has me on my back now and almost split in two—you know, like, dropped down there into the floor section and no way I can get to my feet, my air's getting all cut off—and him punching away at me. All I can see before I pass out is that look in the guy's eyes as he's smashing my face. His eyes are all . . . well, you just don't forget a thing like that. Not ever.

The MAN *stops for a moment, drifting back to the incident. With a start, he shakes his head and looks back at us.*

MAN   . . . anyway, that's how it started and I know it was stupid, just a stupid thing to say and to be involved in and all that, but what're you gonna do? You can't take it back. Uh-uh, you can't, and all the wishing and praying in the world won't make it okay again, make everything go back to zero and be all right. You're stuck with what you've done and you gotta feel like shit about your part in it forever. Yeah, for all time. Ever and ever. Or like that one guy said, in his poem there . . . with the bird? "Evermore." That's a long time to be sorry about one dumb little thing you did, but that's the way it works, and from then on, that *second*, that's your lot in life. To go walking around and feeling crappy about what you've done and how things ended up and the like. Your part in it. And what happened to your life in the meantime because of it . . . (*Wipes his eyes.*) I mean, look at me . . . what a freaking *tragedy* is this, huh? I'm not kidding ya. Forty-four years old and I leave three kids and a wife behind. She's a homemaker, doesn't have a college degree even, and there's not enough insurance or benefits or any of that shit . . . because I'm invincible, right? I'm *immortal* and in the prime of my life and an American and what the hell's ever gonna happen to me? And then something does, and there you are. You're gone and they're left and that's what all these books, all these many religious books that babble about Heaven and Hell and what happens next, *that's* what they've been going on about. In a second, some split second of time, you're just . . . gone. But, see, you're left to wander around like you're still here and look at all the people who love you crying and trying to figure out how to live now and there's not a thing in the world you can do. Not one. It's like being behind that smoky glass in the department store, you know, where, like, the security guys hide and watch you? It's a little bit like that. Where no one can ever see you again but you gotta watch all the outcome of what you did—family having to sell the house and that other guy going to jail for a while (I wasn't so bothered by that!) and your kids *cringing* every time somebody asks 'em about that day . . . that is what you leave behind. *That's* what you get for opening your big mouth about some man's kid who for a few minutes there you forgot is loved by this guy and he'll do anything to make sure that boy grows up strong and happy and secure . . . *any*thing. And that's when you sit down somewhere, in this in-between place where you now find yourself, and you get sick . . . actually physically sick wishing so hard that you could just go back, go back for a second is all, and keep your big mouth shut and watch the game and go get pizza after and fall asleep next to your wife just one more time. Just once. But you can't, no, you can't ever do that again because you forgot that it's a game, it's only a game, and that's something that will haunt you forever and ever and ever . . .

The MAN *sits now, waiting. Alone. The light has slowly begun to fade until only the* MAN'S *face is illuminated.*

MAN   I know it's hard, believe me, I *know* . . . with the mortgage and people on the road driving like maniacs and that new dude at work who's making you crazy, it's so damn hard to remember to just relax and lighten up and take those moments of pleasure that come to you—take 'em and hold 'em close to your chest and just, you know . . . just *squeeze* the shit out of 'em because they are so goddamn precious

. . . but try, okay? That's all I'm gonna say to you about it, is try. *Try*, okay? You try . . . (*Smiles wearily.*) Because it's only a game. It really is. It's a game. That's all. A game. A *game* . . . it's just a game . . . it's . . . just . . .

He trails off as the light on his face finally begins to go—his eyes, the last we see of him, are haunted. He stares out at us.

Silence. Darkness.

romance

production history

Romance had its world premiere in July 2010 in the "Summer Shorts" series at 59E59 in New York City, in a production directed by Andrew McCarthy.

The text was developed in July 2009 at Sala Beckett in Barcelona, Spain.

Neil LaBute

characters

PERSON A   a man or a woman, age can vary

PERSON B   a man or a woman, age can vary

setting

A's home. Near the sea.

time

Now.

NOTE: *Romance* was written as an exercise during an acting workshop in Spain. The four actors and four actresses involved used the text to explore the limits of gender and power on the stage. Any actor can play either role as the material was specifically written without gender—the new dynamic in each performance is brought to the surface by who that actor is and what they try to achieve with their given character.

It made for a wonderful week with a terrific bunch of Catalan actors—I hope it's as fun to play as it was to create.

Silence. Darkness.

Person ("A") sitting alone at a table. After a moment, another person ("B") arrives. Stands. Waits.

A moment passes. A finally sees B. Reacts.

A   . . . oh my God. I mean . . . oh my God.

B   I know.

A   Okay, so . . . like, ummmm, oh-my-God. (*Beat.*) What're you doing here?

B   I dunno. I'm just, you know . . . here.

A   No. No, no, uh-uh, that's not, ummmm . . .

B   I mean . . . I'm not sure why I came.

A   Don't say that. All right? Because *that* is not true. *Whyever* the . . . fuck . . . you're at this place now, with me . . . it's not 'cause you just stumbled in here . . . walked past and went, "Oh, hey, this is quite a surprise." (*Beat.*) You know *exactly* what this is . . .

B   . . . *no* . . .

A   A fucking sneak attack! Okay?! That's what you're doing . . .

B   It's not! No. I am not. (*Beat.*) Listen, I just . . .

A   I mean, you show up here, where I live, and I look up and, and you're just standing there . . . all quiet and just staring. (*Beat.*) *Serial killers* do that kinda shit, all right? Just so you know . . .

B   I'm not here to kill you.

A   Oh, well, good. That's a *relief* . . .

B   Hey, don't say that so easily.

A   What?

B   About me not being in a state to do that. To you. Because I'm . . . yeah.

A   Was that even approaching a sentence?

B takes a slightly threatening step toward A. Leaning in.

B   Shut up, just . . . *shut* up! Okay? Shut up and listen for once . . . just *listen*.

A Fine, God . . .

B I'm saying it's not a crazy thought, the idea of me killing you . . . or hurting you, in some way. It's really not. People have killed each other for less . . . they have.

A Is that right?

B Probably. Less than what *you've* done, anyway. (*Beat.*) You know that's true . . .

A Oh. I see. Now you're gonna go and drag the "truth" into it. (*Beat.*) Okay, fine.

B Yeah, fine.

A All right, so, go on then . . . (*Waits.*) Go.

B What?

A Do it. What you came here to do. Get on with it. (*Checks watch.*) I've got to meet someone at four . . .

B Ha! No surprise there . . .

A What's that?

B Nothing.

A No, go ahead. Make your joke. They're so rare from you that I didn't recognize it at first . . . what you were doing.

B . . . you haven't changed. Not one bit.

A Why would I?

B *Why*?

A No, I mean it. What's wrong with me?

B Ha! You want a list?

A That's the second time you've done that. "Ha!" It doesn't really work for you, so I'd try something else . . . (*Beat.*) "List" of what? My failings?

B Something like that, yeah . . .

A Then go for it . . . if that makes you happy.

B *Happy*?

A That is what I said. "Hap-py."

B You think I'm *happy* doing this? Having to get off work, coming here to this . . . *place* where you're hiding out so I can . . .

A Hey, hey, hey! I'm not doing that. Hiding out. Uh-uh.

B Ummmmm, seems like it to me.

A Well, then, that's you, but us not being in contact—you not

having my details, my *home address*—doesn't make me a
bandit up in the hills, okay? I'm here because I want to be.
I *like* it here . . .

B Whatever.

A Exactly. That's exactly right.

B I had to really search, I mean, I've come a *long* way to speak
to you. Confront you.

A I see. (*Beat.*) So, you want to *confront* me with something
now? Really? Is that it?

B Yeah, that's part of it—I've got some questions for you, and a
few other . . .

A I thought we did this bullshit . . . *months* ago. Last year.
Didn't we? I thought we said our "goodbyes" and you and I
went our separate ways and that was how it goes . . .

B Okay, yes! We did that. I mean, yes . . .

A So, then?

B Then . . . I found this. *Here.*

B *pulls a wrinkled photo out of a pocket. Holds it out. After one
moment* A *takes it and looks at it. Studies it.*

A Fuck.

B That's what I thought. When I saw it . . .

A I had no idea . . .

A *glances at the photo again. Turns it from side to side.*

B . . . neither did *I.* (*Beat.*) It was in the newspaper.

A No. *Really?* Although that makes . . . 'cause I was gonna say,
I have no idea—none—where this came from. (*Beat.*) Wow.

B Yeah. Wow.

Silence between them as A *returns the photo.* B *is about to say
something but* A *cuts in first.*

A And did you have to . . . you know . . . ?

B No, what?

A I mean, aren't you "with" someone now? I thought I heard that recently, that you had met some person and you were pretty serious. Is that not . . . ?

B It's true. (*Beat.*) I mean it's sort of an "open" relationship, but . . . I'm trying it.

A Good for you. Nice.

B Don't. Please.

A What, I can't be happy for you? Is that impossible for us now, to even care about the other person?

B No, but it's just . . . I'm not comfortable talking about that. With you . . . (*Beat.*) And yes, I lied to come here. I had to . . . *and* to my job, about all of this.

A Why?

B Because they wouldn't understand! What do you think? *God* . . .

B waits a moment for this statement to settle in with A.

B So, yes, I made up a lie. I had a "death" in the family . . .

A I see.

B No you don't. You never "see" anything . . . that's part of your problem.

A Well . . . pity you had to lie about coming here. That's always the beginning of the end, I think . . . for relationships, anyway.

B . . . you oughta know.

A Yes. It's true. I oughta.

B Ha! (*That laugh again.*) Ha!

A Please don't start that again . . . your . . .

B Stop.

A *You* stop.

B Fine, I'll . . . just . . . (*Beat.*) I only wanted to understand this whole . . . our past. That's all.

A Why? How could that possibly matter now?

B It just does. (*Beat.*) You were the one who left, so off you go, out the door, and I'm left to pick up the, you know, deal with all the shit that comes with that. Being dumped, and duped, and, and—you *used* me!

A Hey, come on now, that's a little . . .

B No, I *know* you did and . . . (*Pointing.*) I'm not pointing any fingers here, but . . .

A Yes, you are!

B Okay, yes, I guess I am doing that, true, but I'm just *saying* it, okay? As a figure of speech . . . so . . .

A All right, fine . . . (*Beat.*) I have to meet up with someone later, you do remember that, right?

B Yeah . . .

A So can we just . . . ? (*Beat.*) I don't really want to talk about the past.

B . . . fine. Typical, but fine.

B *holds out the photo again, followed by a silent shrug of the shoulders. Searching for an answer.*

A What paper was it in?

B Why, you wanna order a copy?

A Ha! There, how do *you* like it? (*Beat.*) I was just curious, that's all . . .

B I don't know. It was some back issue of the evening paper. Any of our friends or family could've seen it, stumbled onto it at the dentist or wherever—*recycling box* in the garage, like I did, yet I never heard a thing about it, all while we were . . . *nothing!* Isn't that strange? That nobody we know would've seen it or, or . . .

A Maybe they did.

B What? (*Considers this.*) No . . . that's not . . . no way. *No.*

A I'm saying that they could've and just didn't wanna get involved. It's possible.

B No . . . not the kind of person that I'm . . . not my brother or, or, like, our next-door neighbors or . . . I mean, look at you! (*Points to the photo.*) What you're doing!

A I can see the picture. With the fireworks and all the . . . yeah. I see it.

B So, you don't deny that it's you?

A No . . .

B   Huh. Okay. Didn't expect that so easily . . . but . . .

A   I mean, it's pretty obvious. Right? Look at the thing—it's obviously me and I'm doing that, so no, I can't deny it . . .

B   Well, good. Just so we're on the same . . .

A   *Yes.* Crystal. Clear. Got it. Thank you.

B *nods and steps away, thinking for a moment. Turns back.*

B   So . . . (*Beat.*) Do you even care to explain yourself?

A   . . . oh fuck . . .

B   *What?* It's a pretty legitimate question! I mean, this is *years* before we were . . . we broke up last year, in October. Said you needed your freedom, so I . . . I . . . bent over backward to make that work. To be *hip* to that. But no . . . no, then it was something else! The loss of desire. You just didn't want me anymore. Isn't that how you put it? "The spark's gone."

A   Why do this to yourself? Hmmm? And now, when you're with someone who you . . . why?

B   I dunno! I just need to. I saw this and I've been carrying it around and I'm . . . I just *have* to know. That's all.

A   How long were we together? You and me?

B   That doesn't matter—I'm asking you to . . .

A   How many years?

B   Five, I guess. Almost.

A   And the picture is dated what, four years ago? Something like that?

B   Yeah. A little more now . . . (*Looks.*) Yes.

A   Okay, fine. Roughly four years . . . so what does that tell you? *Hmmm?*

B   Shit, I dunno! I-do-not-know, so I'm asking . . .

A   It's me in the photo, yes? Me kissing someone, right on the mouth. *Yes?* Four-years-ago. (*Beat.*) What else do you want me to . . . ?

B   *I'm sorry!* How 'bout that? How about you starting there and see where it gets you! "I am so, *so* fucking sorry that I was an absolute and utter asshole to you during our time together"— try *that* on for size!

A If that's what you need to hear, then okay, yes, I'm sorry.

B But . . . you're not! You aren't, are you?

A No. Not really.

B No, because you've never been sorry! About anything you've ever done in your life. Have you?

A . . . not really. No.

B That's *frightening* . . .

A Yeah, but not sociopathic. At least it's not that. (*Beat.*) . . . I went to a therapist once and they assured me it's mostly just plain old narcissism . . .

B People'll say anything if they can charge you for it.

A Oh, I didn't get charged. We were fucking each other by that point . . .

B Who?! You and the therapist?

A Yeah. So . . .

B . . . oh, that's great . . .

A I'm just saying, it might not've been a *professional* opinion. That could've just been pillow talk.

B You're amazing . . . really . . .

A Hey, I'm just trying to live my life. Okay? That's all I've ever been doing and now I am trying to do it honestly. Without any other person getting hurt or caught in, you know . . . the, ummmm, crossfire. (*Beat.*) I was not a good partner to you, I see that now.

B Ha! (*Beat.*) Sorry, but, no, you weren't . . .

A I just said that . . . (*Beat.*) I'm now aware that I need to be around people who don't threaten me. Strangers. That's how I move these days . . . one-timers. No strings. Just fuck and run . . .

B I'm sorry, but it's a little hard to learn that someone you cared about—no, loved, I *loved* you and I'm still not afraid to say it—that this person was so brazenly living a double life with you, for years before the relationship ended. I mean . . . for years and years and *years* probably!

A Fine, your point is made . . . I was a shit.

B Yes. You were. *And* led me on . . .

A Okay, now this is . . . no, we're not gonna go there. To the next stage. The blame game.

B I'm not, I am not doing that, I'm just . . .

A . . . what do you want? Hmmm? Like, a *quart* of blood or something? I mean . . . *please.* Fuck. Come on. Be a grown-up. Say what it is you want and let's . . . just . . .

B I am!

A No, you're not . . . This is not adult-type behavior here, what you're displaying.

B It is too! Yes, it is! *Yes!*

B stamps one foot on the ground like a child—for a moment, B has a little tantrum. A can only watch.

A I can't give you the time back, all right? It's gone. Both of us, no matter who was doing what to whom, those years are now officially gone. *Poof!* They are behind us and we better keep on moving, otherwise we are gonna look up and be, like, *sixty* and still talking about this shit! (*Beat.*) I'm truly sorry—and I mean it this time—I'm *sorry* but I'm a different person now.

B Are you? Really?

A Yes. I am.

B Well, maybe I should come to your meeting. Come at four and ask if that's the case . . .

A You want to ask my *tax* guy if I'm now a better person, you go right ahead . . .

B You're not meeting an *accountant!* No, you said that . . . you said . . .

A I said I had a *meeting.* At four. Please.

B . . . oh.

A See? This was one of our other problems. *This.* Do you remember? Your neediness . . . You did a couple things on your own that would've made most people drive their car straight into a brick wall, okay?! All the questions and the *pleading* and, and . . .

B *I* believed in what we had! I did, but you never had any desire or hope of it going further. Did you?

A   You mean to, like, a *ceremony* and babies and that sort of . . .
    No. I didn't.
B   But you made me . . . I felt like . . . (*Beat.*) I always thought
    we'd be together forever. In the beginning, anyway. I really did
    believe that.
A   There's no such thing as "forever" anymore. Or "romance."
    Romance is dead . . . There's just today. That's all. To-day.

B *turns to the photo, studying it.* A *looks on with some interest.*

A   And that picture you've got there? I am sorry that you found
    that—that it ever got taken—but I honestly didn't know . . . I
    had *no* idea that we were . . . being . . .
B   I remember this holiday. You told me you had to fly to Rome a
    day early for some—I don't even recall it now. A conference.
    Something.
A   Yes.
B   But that's not . . . (*Looks at picture.*) You weren't in Rome.
A   No. I was about ten miles from the house. At a hotel near the
    beach with . . . I don't know! (*Points.*) *That* person. Whom I
    can't for the life of me remember.
B   And you were kissing . . .
A   Yes.
B   And other stuff, I suppose.
A   No doubt.
B   . . . okay.
A   Okay?
B   I'm just . . . I needed to ask.
A   And that's it? We're done with all the . . . you know . . . the
    begging and the crying . . .
B   Yeah. I don't wanna know any more.
A   All right.
B   I mean, I'm sure if this one ended up in the news that it
    wasn't the first. (*Beat.*) No doubt there's a fucking *club* out
    there somewhere. Right?

A *shrugs at this.* B *shakes it off, laughs out loud.*

B Ha! Anyone else? I mean, while we're at the crossroads here . . . anybody else you need to come clean on? No one? My *sister*?

A Hey, hey! Let's be clear here—this is me doing you a favor. Okay? And no . . . not your sister. (*Beat.*) Not that she didn't ask . . .

B What?! You fucking liar!

A Okay, I'm lying . . .

B That is bullshit! Not in a *million* years!

A I don't wanna do this now. Please?

B No, tell me! Tell me! *Tell me!*

A *Twice.* Offered, never acted upon.

B Fuck. I mean . . . fuck! That is . . . *so* . . .

A I didn't ask you to come here, remember? To dig through this again, so just keep that in mind while you're getting all . . .

B I mean . . . fuck! My *sister*.

A All I can do is report this shit, I am not responsible. (*Beat.*) For that one, at least . . .

Silence again for a moment while B *regroups.* A *waits.*

B Okay, that's probably enough. I mean . . . I'm starting to . . . I feel a little sick.

A Do you need anything? I think I have an aspirin somewhere.

B No, I'm fine. I just need to get back to my hotel. Lie down and . . . and . . .

A Where're you staying?

B What? Oh . . . at the Beverly, I think it's called. Something like that. Right there in the center of town.

A I know the one. With all the . . . it's nice.

B Yeah, I'm sure you fucked somebody there. Right?

A Probably. (*Beat.*) You're a little obsessed with this . . . aren't you?

B I don't know what I am. I'm all . . . shit. I dunno. (*Beat.*) What did you mean just now?

A What?

B Before, when you said . . . You cut yourself off before you could say it. Something.

A . . . no . . .

B Yes! Something about—what were you gonna say? "For that one, at least." *That* one, so more than one, right? Obviously. More than, like . . . than . . .

A *Aggghhh!* Let's not do this again!

B No, I wanna hear you, what you were . . .

A . . . come on, please don't . . .

B *Say it!* You almost did, you were going to say how many, so say it. Go on, do me the favor. (*Beat.*) *Please.* I'm asking nicely.

Silence as A *thinks about this.* B *watches as* A *considers.*

A . . . all right then. You might wanna sit.

B *does so.* A *waits for this to happen and then talks.*

A This is the story as I remember it: You always liked me. A lot more than I ever liked you, but it was a good, solid deal between the two of us, so I went along with it. With us being seen as *together* and all of that—but I was never faithful to you. Not one day. I was out with someone or chasing the next one, calling them from the other room while you were in the shower . . . from *literally* the first day I moved in. Right from then on. You were easy . . . easy to live with, lie to, all that, but I wasn't attracted to you: *yet* I realized, after a while, anyway, that it was okay to let the sex die out, to shudder to a stop and we could still . . . *bumble* along as a couple. So I did. I did that—continued to see whomever I wanted . . . whenever I wanted to, and use our place as my home base, a spot to launch from in my pursuit of endless pleasure. (*Beat.*) *But*, at some point, and I'm not sure why—I think I woke up to the sound of you crying one night, that may have been it—I finally needed out. It felt wrong and so I told you I had to go. It was a mercy killing, me breaking up with you. It was me helping you dodge a bullet . . . (*Beat.*) That picture there is just minor evidence of the truth, the *tip* of the fucking iceberg of who I was and so I left and that was that. I am sorry that I hurt you. Used you. *Damaged* you, even, in some way. That was bad of me. I grew up—a little, anyway—and realized that I should just go out and get whatever I wanted *but* live a truthful life. And so I did. I set you free and that must be some kind of love, isn't it? I dunno, but I'm happy now. I am, and all I hope is that you can be, too . . .

Silence sets in as A *and* B *simply look at each other.*

B   . . . I hate you. I really do. I absolutely hate you. And yet . . . I still *want* you, or, or . . . I dunno. Something. (*Beat.*) I won't ask you how you feel about me.

A   That's probably best.

B   I can't . . . even now that I'm with someone else, in spite of that . . . I long for your kisses. Your caress. (*Beat.*) I'm here, in front of you with all this *hatred* inside me but I would jump at the chance to be with you again . . . Oh, God . . .

A   Huh. Well, maybe we should . . . It's getting close to four.

B   I know you have to go, I know that, but I'm . . . I just . . . (*Beat.*) Listen, would you meet me later? At my hotel?

A   I don't know that I can. Or even should.

B   Just *once*. That's what you do now. Isn't it? One-timers, you said so yourself.

A   I know, but . . . that's . . .

B   And if there were ever two people more estranged from each other—*strangers*—I can't imagine who.

A   That's true.

B   We can just lie there if you want to . . . side by side. We don't have to do things. Not if . . . (*Beat.*) . . . But will you meet me?

A   I'm . . . I dunno. (*Beat.*) Yeah . . . I guess I will. Yes.

B   And touch me, maybe. And let me do it to you, too? Is that possible?

A   Yes, it is. It's possible.

B   Thank you.

A But what about . . . you know? Your new . . . ?

B I don't care.

A It'd be cheating. Sort of. *Technically.*

B Then I'll cheat. I've never done it to a person I've loved but I would with you . . .

A That's sweet. (*Beat.*) So I'll . . . yes. I'll try to swing by.

B You will?

A Yeah. A bit later. When it's dark . . .

B Perfect.

A Uh-huh. Yep. (*Beat.*) I need to go now.

B Okay, I understand. I'll be waiting . . . Even if you don't come, I'll be waiting for you.

A Promise?

B I do.

A Then good, that's nice. It is. Thank you . . .

B . . . you're welcome.

A walks off. Looks back once and then is gone. B *watches* A *go, then turns to the picture. Pulls it close. Kisses it once. Then again. Then still again.*

A tongue finally erupts through the paper. Twirling and pink and twisting about.

Silence. Darkness.

the

furies

production history

The Furies had its world premiere in September 2008 at *Eating Their Words* in New York in a production directed by Marlo Hunter.

Neil LaBute

characters

BARRY   a man in his forties
JIMMY   a man in his mid-twenties
JAMIE   a woman in her late twenties

setting

A well-appointed restaurant in the midtown area.

time

Today.

NOTE: *The Furies* also exists in a non-same-sex version where "Barry" becomes "Paula" and the issues at hand become slightly different. If this is of interest, please contact the author via the Gersh Agency in New York City for details.

A slash in dialogue denotes a suggested point of overlap between that line and the next actor's line.

Silence. Darkness.

A man sitting at a table, waiting. He sips at a coffee and steals a glance at his watch. After a bit, he pulls a note out of an opened envelope and scans it. Returns it to the envelope, then replaces the whole thing in his sport jacket.

This is BARRY.

There is a smart-looking dessert in front of him—some kind of mousse and fruit and God-knows-what. He steals a taste.

Another moment goes by. Suddenly a young man appears next to the table. A young woman at his side. They wear similar terse expressions and are dressed for the heat. With a long sigh the young man sits down at the table. Young woman follows. This is JIMMY *and his sister,* JAMIE.

BARRY   . . . oh. (*Beat.*) Hi. / That's . . . hey, there. *Guys.*

JIMMY   Hey. / Yeah, hi.

BARRY   So. What's up?

JIMMY   I dunno. You called me.

BARRY   I know, but . . . I'm . . . I didn't mean for . . .

JIMMY   You called and said you wanted to meet, so, you know, here I am.

BARRY   Uh-huh. With . . .

JIMMY   You said we should meet tonight, so I dropped everything and came running—called in sick for work and I shot over here. / To see you.

BARRY   Good. / Okay, that's great . . . I mean . . .

JIMMY   Sure. Of course. (*Beat.*) You still mean the world to me, so . . .

BARRY   Thank you.

JIMMY   I mean, you do, you *totally* do, and some little thing like us having an argument is not gonna drastically change that. You know? / It's not.

BARRY Sure. / Of course. (*Beat.*) It was a pretty big fight, though, I mean, just to be completely . . . you know . . .

JIMMY leans over as JAMIE whispers something in his ear.

JIMMY That's how *I* feel, anyway—even if you can't possibly say something nice to me in return.

BARRY I see. (*Beat.*) And why did you bring your sister with you? Just curious.

JIMMY Backup. / For backup.

BARRY Oh. / But that's . . . Why?

JIMMY To back me up, just in case . . .

BARRY In case what?

JIMMY You know. *In case.* You go all weird on me here . . .

BARRY That's not . . . (*Turns to JAMIE.*) No offense, Jamie, but I'd really like to talk to Jim on my own. Discuss a few things.

JAMIE whispers into JIMMY's ear again.

JIMMY Tough shit. (*Beat.*) That's not me, she said that. "Tough shit." / Jamie did.

BARRY Ahh. / Well, that's nice. *Sweet.*

JIMMY Jamie's very straightforward about stuff.

BARRY Yeah, I get that . . . / Right.

JIMMY Always has been. / Just her way—and I trust her, okay?

BARRY Fine.

JIMMY I do. / She's my sister, my *rock*. She's my . . . my . . . you know. She's that.

BARRY I said "fine." / O-kay, Jim, it's fine. I get it.

Silence for a moment as they sit. BARRY takes another bite of the dessert.

BARRY Would you like some? Hmm? / It's got mango . . . I know you like the . . .

JIMMY No, that's okay. / Nope. No thanks.

BARRY Sure? It's, like, *twelve* calories . . . it's not even cream there. All that stuff on the . . . it's some kind of a *mousse.* (*Beat.*) No? All right. I was just . . . Anyway, how've you been?

JIMMY Good. Pretty much.

BARRY That's nice.

JIMMY Yep. You?

BARRY Ummm, you know . . . just going along. Still trying to firm up some kind of rapport with my kids, and, and I mean, just . . . building bridges. Mostly. Trying to repair a lot of the relationships that got torn apart when I . . . you know. First came out.

JIMMY No, I mean since Thursday. (*Whisper from* JAMIE.) Sorry. Two weeks ago, *two* Thursdays since we had our . . . whatever.

BARRY Right.

JIMMY Since then.

BARRY I remember.

JIMMY The "fight." Our little blowout . . .

BARRY No, I get what you . . . yes.

Another whisper from JAMIE *into* JIMMY's *ear.*

JIMMY Which *you* started. (*Beat.*) That's just her opinion—she wasn't even there, she's just lashing out—but still . . .

BARRY Sure. Still.

JIMMY You been okay? / Good. That's . . .

BARRY Yes. Okay. / I'm . . . no, actually . . . Look, I'm not feeling . . .

JIMMY What?

BARRY Good. I am not that . . . all right. I've been . . . I think a lot of the last however many months that we were together, I've been . . .

JIMMY . . . we're *still* together . . .

BARRY Yeah, I know, I'm just saying . . .

JIMMY We had a *tiff* . . . We took some time, some "alone" time—that's what you called it and I agreed to it—but we didn't break up. / I mean, not so far as *I* knew . . .

the furies

BARRY No. / No, that's true, but . . . I'm . . .

That whisper again. JIMMY *stares right at* BARRY. JAMIE *covers her mouth but gestures with the other hand (this is a habit of hers throughout).*

JIMMY Unless you're trying to pull something. (*A whisper.*) Which it seems like . . . to Jamie, that is. Me, I'm trying to keep an open mind. (*Beat.*) So what did you wanna say?

BARRY . . . nothing.

JIMMY No, go ahead.

BARRY Not now, I can't now, I'm . . . (*Beat.*) Would you like to— *either* of you—do you want to order some dinner or anything? / Coffee?

JIMMY I'm good. / I had food already.

BARRY Fine. That's . . .

More whispers from JAMIE *to* JIMMY. *Silent arguing.*

JIMMY Jamie'll have the nachos. (*Whisper.*) "Grande," but no olives. I mean, if you're okay with that . . .

BARRY I don't . . . not sure they do *nachos* here. / Judging from the, ummm . . .

JIMMY Okay. / Fine. (*Whisper.*) If that's how you wanna play it. / What?

JAMIE *whispers into* JIMMY'*s ear again. At intervals.*

BARRY It's not me! I mean, look around at the . . . / It's not really that kind of place. For nachos. (*Beat.*) Does she . . . ?

JIMMY What?

BARRY Nothing. / It's nothing . . .

JIMMY No, go ahead. / *What?*

BARRY Does she have to do that? All that, you know . . . the "whispering" thing?

JIMMY She has polyps on her vocal cords, you know that . . . / You *already* know that! Jesus.

BARRY No, I know . . . / I do, yes. Sorry.

JIMMY It's serious . . . a totally serious condition.

BARRY I'm sure.

JIMMY *Totally.* She hasn't been able to sing with her band for almost *six* weeks . . . I mean, they have gigs on, like, most weeknights and she's . . .

BARRY I'm sorry. (*To her.*) Sorry, Jamie.

JIMMY You know what it's like to stand out onstage every night and only be able to shake your *tambourine*? / Huh?

BARRY No, I don't. / I'm sure it's . . .

JIMMY It's hell, that's what it is. (*The whisper.*) A "living" hell, all right? So maybe take it a little easy on my sister . . . (*Whisper.*) Who was also raised to have manners.

BARRY Oh. Sorry. I always thought whispering was bad manners . . .

JIMMY No.

BARRY It's not?

JIMMY No, not if you're— (*Whisper.*) Ever heard of "speak when spoken to"?

BARRY I have, yes.

JIMMY All right, then.

BARRY Right. (*To* JAMIE.) Would you like to try something else? My dessert?

JAMIE *turns away in a huff.* JIMMY *watches this. He sighs.*

JIMMY Guess not. (*Beat.*) So what did you wanna say to me?

BARRY Ahh—I just spoke to her. Does that not count? I mean, what about her "speak when spoken to" thing?

JIMMY I told you already! She's got that throat condition . . . *God.* / Is it so, so important that she responds to the *nacho* issue right now? Huh?

BARRY Sorry. / No. 'Course not. (*Beat.*) This is not how I was hoping . . . and it's not an issue, okay? It's not some . . . they just don't have them. That's all.

JIMMY Is this what you brought me here for? To beat up on my family? (*The whisper.*) Who never did anything to you . . .

(*Whisper.*) . . . but be nice and kind . . . (*Whisper.*) . . . and even
took you canoeing that one Sunday when you complained that
we never do . . .

BARRY   Okay! I'm sorry. I'm so sorry for me bringing it up. Really.
/ *Sorry.*

JIMMY   I mean, seriously. / *Why* am I here? This was an overtime
shift, you know, and that's good money . . .

BARRY   No, I know, and I appreciate that.

JIMMY   Fine. / That's cool.

BARRY   I do. / Honestly. I do, Jim. (*Beat.*) Your family has been
a lot more . . . *open* to us—our relationship—than mine ever
was. That's true, Jim.

Another quick whisper from JAMIE *to her brother.*

JIMMY   I know you don't care for it, but most people do call me
"Jimmy," okay, and I like it. / Just so you know.

BARRY   Sorry. "Jimmy." / Right.

A long pause. BARRY *is obviously nervous to get this started.*

BARRY   Look—there's no good way to start this—I needed to
see you again, to get some things straight before I go and . . .
I mean "us," before we . . .

JIMMY   . . . here it comes. / The thing.

BARRY   What? / What "thing"?

JIMMY   You know. The *thing.* The weird part that I mentioned
before—where you take a little misunderstanding we had
and blow it out of proportion so that I get all frustrated and
angry and I finally say, I say . . . "Fine, you're right, no, you are
absolutely right!" And we break up. You'll push me to break
this off when all along that's probably what you wanted. It's
your idea but you use me, you do some bad trick like that to
make it seem like I'm the evil, unthinking . . . mean-spirited
one. (*Beat.*) That is how this shit works. / I watch TV.

BARRY   Wow. / God, that's . . . ahhhh . . .

JIMMY   What?

BARRY   Nothing, no, that's just . . . that's very *elaborate.*

JIMMY   What is?

BARRY   That plan. I'm saying if that's what I was doing, doing a
thing like that to you—well, it's just quite a deal you cooked
up there. In your head.

JIMMY   Hey, I've had two *weeks* to think about it. (*Whisper.*)
Thanks to you.

BARRY   Right. Okay, so, I'm . . . Listen, what needs to happen
here, and I very much did want to do this in private . . . (*To*
JAMIE.) No offense, Jamie, but—you need to know a few
things, okay? I mean, at least one thing, a *big* thing, that I've
been . . . that I probably should've been more clear about
since I was, well, ever since I was first made aware of it.

JIMMY   All right. / Go then, I'm ready . . .

BARRY   You need to know this. / I'm . . . this is very hard . . .

Another whisper from JAMIE. *She glances over at* BARRY *as she
does it. The slightest smile on* JIMMY's *face afterward.*

JIMMY   Just say it . . . / Jamie called it before, anyway.

BARRY   I'm trying to . . . / Called what?

JIMMY   You're going back, right? To your wife, I mean. That's
what you're trying to . . . / I didn't believe her when she first
said it either, but now, hey—makes sense.

BARRY   What? / No! No, I'm not getting back together with her or
. . . no, I'm not.

JIMMY   You sure?

BARRY   Yes! Or anything like that—which would be fine if that's
what I was doing, of course it would be, if that's what I
wanted, but—I don't.

JIMMY   Seriously, you can tell us. (*Beat.*) She's pregnant, isn't
she? That's what it is . . . she got you drunk and now the slut
is *pregnant*, right?!

BARRY   No! She did not do anything like that, at all. Ever. *No.*

JIMMY   'Kay. (*Whisper.*) Positive? / It would explain a lot . . .

BARRY I'm positive! / My God, every time we argue about . . .
*any*thing, you say I'm running back to my wife . . . or that I'm
not really gay, or . . . Why are we doing this?! I mean, *please!*

JIMMY You tell me! (*Beat.*) Jamie gave up a gig for this . . .

BARRY Oh, I'm sorry! I am *so* sorry there, Jamie, that I ruined an
evening for you . . . really. *Forgive* me.

JAMIE *stares* BARRY *down, then turns and whispers in* JIMMY*'s ear.*

JIMMY She doesn't think that you're being sincere—and I gotta
say, with that tone . . .

BARRY Jim, stop! *Jimmy*, whatever. Do not say any more, okay?
No more stupid . . . crap out of your mouth today now . . . so,
just listen.

JIMMY . . . hey, I'm trying to be all . . .

BARRY *holds up a hand to his mouth, makes that "zip it" motion,
and points right at* JIMMY.

BARRY *No.* You're done. (*Beat.*) Look, you can bring your sister
along and, and make me . . . *try* and make me feel crazy, like
I'm being all silly or something, but now you're gonna shut up
and listen to me. (*Holds up his hand as she whispers.*) *Stop.*
Really—both of you—I need to say this and you're gonna hear
it. All right?

JIMMY Fine. Jesus, whatever—be a psycho.

BARRY Jimmy! Shut-up. Listen. Zip those lips and *listen* to me.
(*Beat.*) I'm dying. There. You hear that? I am dying . . .

JIMMY . . . oh. / I mean . . . what? *What*?

BARRY Yeah. / Yes. I'm gonna die.

JIMMY You . . . you're shitting me . . .

BARRY I wish. (*Beat.*) I am in the process of dying. I've got about
six weeks if I'm . . . if I get lucky or, or . . .

JIMMY That's . . . my God . . . oh my . . .

BARRY Exactly. Yes. "My God." (*To* JAMIE.) Did you wanna say
anything?

JAMIE *turns her head away.* JIMMY *glances at his sister, then speaks again.*

JIMMY But you're . . . What does that mean?

BARRY What does it usually mean? Death.

JIMMY I know, but . . .

BARRY I have a . . . I've been diagnosed with a fairly rare—a *disorder*. It's not AIDS, and *no*, I don't think it's a curse or a plague or, like, payback for my—it's a disease, that's all. One that is going to . . . eat away at my . . . it's going to . . . you know . . . up there. Up inside me. (*Motions.*) *Up.*

BARRY's *voice breaks. He fights back tears.* JIMMY *takes his hand and* JAMIE *turns, staring at him. He backs off a little.*

JIMMY Barry, I'm . . . shit, I'm so sorry.

BARRY It's okay.

JIMMY I had no idea . . . I mean, none!

BARRY Of course not, I know that . . . How could you?

JIMMY I really didn't. (*Beat.*) I mean, I never could've guessed a thing like that . . . Barry . . . *baby* . . . oh-my-God!

BARRY It's so . . . *I'm* sorry it took me this long to say something but I've been a little . . . it's just been really . . . it's *hard*, you know?

JIMMY Of course! Sure, of course it is . . .

BARRY It's almost impossible to wrap your own head around it and so then when you know that you have to share it with . . . *others* . . . it takes a kind of strength that I didn't really have at the time . . .

JIMMY Absolutely. I understand.

JAMIE *finally reacts to all this—whispering in her brother's ear. What a surprise.*

JIMMY How long have you known?

BARRY I'm sorry?

JIMMY Jamie's just curious—she feels bad, I mean, look at her, but—she just wondered. How long. (*Beat.*) So?

BARRY *studies* JAMIE *but can't read her blank expression. She looks at* JIMMY*, then nudges him. He turns back to* BARRY.

BARRY Ummm . . . a few months. Two months, I guess. Almost three.

JIMMY Oh.

BARRY Right around there, anyway . . .

JIMMY I see. Cool.

BARRY I know I should've . . . but it's been a long series of tests and, and, I mean, you can imagine—second opinions, all that. / Pretty horrible, really . . .

JIMMY Of course. / Sure.

BARRY But I didn't wanna worry you and . . . I was scared. Denying it, even to myself. This whole time, I've been fighting it and, and, you know . . . *wrestling* with it. All alone.

JIMMY Makes sense. (*Takes his hand.*) That's really brave of you . . .

BARRY It's a day at a time, you know? 'S all you can do—go forward but just one day at a time.

JIMMY I get that. (*Beat.*) I do wish you'd said something—trusted me enough to share this with you—but I think I understand. / 'Course. (*A whisper.*) What now?

BARRY Thank you, Jim-my. "Jimmy." / Sorry?

JIMMY What do we do now? (*More whispers.*) I'm sure Jamie means "you" but I'm thinking on a bigger scale here . . . globally, as a couple—you and me—what's the best thing to do?

BARRY Oh. (*Beat.*) Ahh . . . well, I think the, I mean, the *only* thing I can really imagine is letting you go. / No. *No.*

JIMMY Breaking up? / What's it mean, then?

BARRY It means setting you free, that's what . . . not dragging someone down who I care about—and you know I do, you know that I care for you, Jim—please let me just use that name for now, I'm a grown-up and I'm used to it—I've cared

about you all during this year or so that we've been going
out . . .

A whisper from JAMIE *again.* JIMMY *leans over and listens.*

JIMMY Fourteen months. I knew that, too, but Jamie's really
good with numbers.
BARRY Right. So, yes, fourteen months . . . That's a long time
and I don't . . . I can't be the kind of person who is selfish
and clinging and, and just a *user* . . . not even in death.
JIMMY I don't think that about you . . .
BARRY No, not now, you just found out . . . so, of course not.
Not yet, but you will. I promise you will and I just can't go
through all this with that on my shoulders, too . . .
JIMMY . . . but . . .
BARRY It just makes sense, Jim! No, think about it . . . we're
not married, we do not have kids . . . (*Puts his hand up.*)
Please let me finish. We are not at all bound here, not legally
. . . and I will always feel connected to you—in my heart,
I'm saying—so the only right thing to do, the moral and true
course of action here is for me to let you go. To dig deep and
bear this thing on my own . . . and with my family, of course—
not Sheryl and the kids . . . not them—but I mean my *parents*
and siblings and all those folks—just take whatever comes.
/ It's the only way. It's the way I was raised.
JIMMY But that's . . . / . . . that's so . . .
BARRY I think it's best. I really do . . . (*Takes a bite.*) You sure
you don't want a taste? Either of you? It's got a crust that's
like . . . *flaky* is too simple a word for it . . . it's . . . some sort
of buttery . . . I dunno . . .

JIMMY *waves it off. Thinking. Staring over at* BARRY, *who takes a
bite through tear-filled eyes.*

JIMMY Oh, man . . . man, man, man! (*Beat.*) I'm not sure that I
. . . I can't even see myself living in a world that you aren't a
part of, Barry.

the furies   121

BARRY Please don't say that—please? I'm not going to be able to . . . I cannot carry that kind of guilt away with me. I need you to be strong. To, to live and be a . . . you're young! Young and so, *so* vibrant . . . you'll be . . .

JIMMY I know, I'm sorry, it's just . . . my head is spinning here, and I'm . . . (*Another of those whispers.*) . . . to where? I don't . . . no, I'm not gonna ask that. *No.*

JAMIE *pulls on* JIMMY's *coat and whispers more in his ear.* JIMMY *shakes his head again "no."*

BARRY Excuse me? What's the . . . ?

JIMMY It's . . . (JAMIE *prods him.*) Fine! (*To* BARRY.) You said carry it "away with me." You mean, like, to your death? The grave or wherever? / Is that . . . ?

BARRY Ummm . . . well, yes. / *Yes.* Eventually.

JIMMY Oh. (*Beat.*) I thought you only had six weeks or so. To go.

BARRY I do. Yes, I do, but that's . . . there is treatment available, which I've planned to . . . you know . . .

JIMMY Here? In town?

BARRY Well, no . . . no, in San Francisco. / Yeah, so that's . . . I'll be . . .

JIMMY Ahh. / I see. That's *convenient.*

BARRY *What?* There are specialists there who . . . I'll probably stay with . . . where they can monitor . . . all my . . .

JIMMY In California. / Nice. Perfect.

BARRY Yes. / It's . . . the best thing for . . .

JIMMY Huh. (*Whisper.*) Where you talked to me about moving. I mean, as a . . .

BARRY It's a *hospital!*

JIMMY . . . then fine . . .

BARRY A sort of hospice where they offer up some relief . . . a momentary . . .

JIMMY It's just that you've said before about—and you have family there . . .

BARRY Yeah, who'll be *burying* me, is that all right?!

JIMMY Please don't talk like that . . .

BARRY Then don't say things . . . *shit* about me . . . being
capable of doing . . .

JIMMY I'm sorry! I'm in a little bit of shock here . . . (*A whisper.*)
And it is where your wife and kids moved, so I'm just saying,
don't be all . . .

BARRY To San Diego! *Hundreds* of miles to the south from where
I'll . . .

JIMMY She's got a car, right? (*Beat.*) *And* if she did manage to
get herself knocked up, then please just say it now and get it
over with, I *beg* you! Honestly, I can take it!

BARRY Come on, please?! *Please* don't do this to me now! Not
now, when I'm trying to . . . (*Beat.*) I am not, *not* going there
for them. To go back to or be with them. I'm going home—to
the Bay Area—to die. To try and get a little relief before I pass
away. (*To* JAMIE.) Is that all right?! Can I have your *permission*
to die?!

JIMMY 'Course. (*Beat.*) And there's not any doctor in town who
can . . . ?

BARRY Oh-my-God. I can't believe that you would . . . / I cannot
believe you'd go there, that you would even . . .

JIMMY What?! / It's just a question . . .

BARRY No! There's no one here capable of this kind of . . . Don't
you think I'd check into that? / Stop! Stop it!!

JIMMY Yeah, but ya have to go *all* the way to . . . ? / I'm just
saying . . .

BARRY Well don't! Do not give voice to a, a, a horrible and
pathetic and, God, just *venal* idea like that . . . (*To* JAMIE.) *My*
mind doesn't work like that. No.

A silence falls over the table for a moment. JIMMY *glances at his
sister, then back to* BARRY.

JIMMY You have to admit, though, people do all kinds of stuff
when they . . .

BARRY What, die?!

JIMMY No, I'm saying—when they find it hard to end something,
a relationship, or some . . .

the furies   123

BARRY Hey, *Jimmy*—fully grown man with a twelve-year-old's name—no offense, but you're not that *special*. Okay? If I wanted to break it off with you I would. I just would.

JIMMY Fine.

BARRY So, yeah. I mean . . . please.

Another silence washes over them—not literally—but it's a very quiet table while both sides regroup.

You knew another whisper was coming from JAMIE. JIMMY *reacts.*

JIMMY No. Absolutely not. (*Whisper.*) You ask it then! Go ahead and . . . (*She pushes him.*) Okay! Shit. You're such a bully . . . (*To* BARRY.) You wouldn't have a . . . it's not, like, written down anywhere, is it?

BARRY I'm not . . . what do you mean?

JIMMY Just, you know . . . the results or a doctor's . . . (*Whisper.*) I'm asking! Any kind of letter that says . . .

BARRY Jesus Christ! *What* is it with you two, huh? Your sister and you? You should spend a couple hours on a doctor's couch trying to figure it out because this is . . . whatever. I don't care. (*Pulls a letter out of his coat.*) Ya know, I almost didn't bring this . . . almost left it at home because I thought, "Nooo . . . not even Jim and his crazy . . . even his creepy family couldn't *possibly* ask me for *documentation* when they hear that I am dying. Once they know my insides are being eaten alive by . . . " Then I popped it in my jacket; I did, tossed it in there because I went, "Yep, actually, if anybody is gonna be sick enough and, and, and *foul* enough to want proof then it will be him . . . him or that pathetic sister of his who follows him around like something out of a bad fifties movie or, or, or like one of those Greek-type dramas where the bloodlines are all screwed up! A someone like *that* just might ask—so here it is.

BARRY *slams the letter down on the table, staring at both of them. Daring them to move.*

BARRY Enjoy.

JIMMY *goes for the note but stops—reaches for* BARRY*'s hand instead. He is crying now and reluctant to give in but he finally does.*

After a moment, JAMIE *takes a peek.* BARRY *sees this and pulls his hand free of* JIMMY*'s grip.*

BARRY I knew it! I *knew* she'd have to . . .

JIMMY Sorry! (*To* JAMIE.) Can ya just leave it? Why don't you go wait for me in the car, okay? (*Whisper.*) I don't care if it's . . . no. Jamie, stop. *Stop.*

BARRY What?

JIMMY Nothing.

BARRY No, I wanna hear this—Jim, I *want* to. (*To* JAMIE.) What?

JIMMY She just . . . the letter. She noticed that the, you know, the letterhead isn't . . . it's not . . .

BARRY Yeah? / So?

JIMMY It's a copy, that's all. / She saw that it's not *embossed* or anything.

BARRY . . . I don't get what you're . . .

JIMMY Nothing, just that . . . she said you can get that right off the website if you wanted to . . . so . . .

BARRY Aaaaahhhhhhh! / Aaaahhhhhhhhhhhh!

JIMMY Barry, I'm sorry! / It's not *me* . . .

BARRY No! Not another word out of you . . . you, you coward! You're *pathetic.* (*To* JAMIE.) I'm so glad that this is happening to me. I really am. Know why? Because I can't wait to leave here, I can't . . . and I don't just mean for California, I'm saying to actually *die.* I-can't-wait! Because if I do survive this, somehow manage to hang on and make it through the injections—which won't happen, they've assured me, it is just pain management at this point—but if I did, then surely, at some point, I'd recover enough to think back, to reflect back on the former life I led with my insane, neurotic boyfriend and his *harpy* of a sister who maybe gave him, like, I dunno, a blow job one summer and now she's got some sort of *Vulcan* mind-lock over him and I don't want that . . . I do not *ever* want to think about the two of you again! (*Beat.*) So, yeah, I cannot wait for me to die. I'll be gone and I will never have to consider your little whisper or your face or, or your . . . disgusting *polyps*—any *part* of you—not ever again. Got it? Hmm?! (*Straight at* JAMIE.) You got that, *Jamie*—girl who loves to call other people all kinds of, of shit but is actually the one sporting what I'd consider a pretty *androgynous* name! *Got-it?* (*Beat.*) Then good.

BARRY *stands to leave, gathers his things.* JAMIE *leans over to whisper in* JIMMY's *ear and that's it—the final straw.* BARRY *throws the dessert right in* JAMIE's *face. It covers her—her clothes, the letter on the table. Everything.*

BARRY   Go to hell, bitch!

The moment is frozen—finally JIMMY *tries to reach out to* BARRY, *who slaps his hand away. He turns to go. As* BARRY *does,* JAMIE *finally speaks. A forced, hoarse whisper; sort of how you'd imagine Medusa sounding when she gets going.*

JAMIE   . . . you better run! *Barr-ee.* You had better pack up your shit and head off to California—and you better die, just like you said you would. (*Beat.*) 'Cause if you don't, I'll find you. I will. I'll make it my life's mission to track you down like one of those bloodhound dogs and I will bite down on your leg and hold ya there until the proper authorities can come along and do to you what needs to be done. To a person like *you*. You old queen . . . I'm so on to you. This—(*makes a big open-armed gesture*)—all of this smells like bullshit and ya can't fool me. For some reason you are running away from him, from this sweet, sweet guy. Jimmy. My brother Jimmy's getting shafted and he may even fall for it . . . may hold your hand and send you *daisies* and cry his eyes out tonight but not me—I'm not gonna believe you until I see the last shovelful of dirt hit your ten-dollar casket. (*Beat.*) And even then I'll probably think you pulled a fast one . . . broke his heart and ran off to the West Coast for whatever reason . . . faked your own death and got back together with that *fag hag* of yours who's willing to overlook all your freaky shit and call herself your wife. *That* is what *I* think.

JAMIE *stops and grabs the empty plate on the table—licks the last of the mousse off of it.* BARRY *scoops up his letter.*

JAMIE Take back your letter, I don't care one little bit. I'll be calling the "Smythson Institute" very soon, and if I don't find you there, coughing up blood or shitting out your *colon* . . . well, let's just say there's gonna be hell to pay . . . (*Beat.*) You called me a lot of bad names there, crap I don't even understand because some of us weren't put through college by their parents, but I do get the gist of it. I do, and that's just what I'm gonna be to you from now on—one of those things from Greek stories or whatever, like you said, that fly around and pick at you . . . pick-pick-pick at your dirty little mind . . . like Jiminy Cricket with a fucking stick up his ass! I will hunt you down and hound you to hell if you don't die or—better yet—I catch you lying about any of this. Oh yes, I will be watching you, so don't think I won't. If I spot even one *Polaroid* of you on your kid's Facebook page that is new or looks suspicious or anything—a *single* mention of you over the Internet in anything other than an obituary—and your ass'll be mine, *baby.*

JAMIE *lets this land for effect—*BARRY*'s eyes widen and* JIMMY *looks over at his sister. Back to* BARRY. *Shakes his head.*

JAMIE Now, my brother may say, "Jamie, let it go, just leave him alone . . . " but not me. Uh-uh. Not now . . . not after what you've said and done and, and *insinuated.* No. Six years from now I'll slip in a side window of your luxury home and I'll proceed to tear your happy little life to shreds. I will slit your children's throats and feed you their *eyes* in a homemade pudding, forcing you to choke down every-last-drop. I will make it my business to find your lovely wife . . . seduce her at yoga and fuck her brains out before disemboweling her with a *pen knife.* A note pinned to her Danskins. A note left just for you . . . Little Mr. Better-Than-Thou, that says: "Now we're even." (*Beat.*) *That's* the kind of momentous shit that is about to rain down on your pathetic head . . . Barry. *If* you are lying to us. / I kid you not.

BARRY You're . . . I mean, that is just . . . / I don't even know what to say to the two of you . . . I'm . . .

JIMMY *reaches out for him but* BARRY *doesn't go to him.* JAMIE *is staring him down.*

JIMMY . . . Barry . . . / Please! / She's just . . .

BARRY No! Don't touch me. / I try to do a good . . . to give you the *benefit* of the . . . / I am *dying* here! *Dying!* What's the matter with you people?! I have to . . . I'm . . . I need to . . .

JAMIE *suddenly stands and starts to move at him—*BARRY *backs up and staggers away. Offstage.* JAMIE *slowly returns to her chair.*

JIMMY *and* JAMIE *sit at the table in silence. Finally,* JIMMY *speaks.*

JIMMY . . . well, that's great. That is just *great!* You happy now? (*Another whisper.*) God, I can't take you anywhere . . .

He looks over at JAMIE, *who is still revved up but doesn't say anything. She looks away. They sit back and wait for something to happen. Brother and sister, alone together.*

Silence. Darkness.

the

war

on

terror

production history

The War on Terror had its world premiere in October 2008 during the "Broken Space" play series at the Bush Theatre in London in a production directed by Neil LaBute.

characters

YOUNG WOMAN   closing in on thirty

YOUNG MAN   somewhere in his thirties

setting

A nondescript sitting room and, ultimately, a small theater.

time

Just yesterday.

NOTE: The spelling in *The War on Terror* has been Americanized to fit with the style of the rest of this collection. The following monologue, however, was originally performed by the English actress Michelle Terry as if the character (and the actress portraying that character) was from London.

While this short play is fictional and meant only to entertain, some members of the Muslim faith may find portions of it offensive. If that is the case, I suggest you write to the author in care of the Gersh Agency in New York City or go burn down an embassy. You decide.

Silence. Darkness.

Lights up slowly to reveal a YOUNG WOMAN *sitting on a chair. Staring down at a military beret in her hands.*

YOUNG WOMAN   . . . this is what's left. Of him. The man I love. This. His unit sent it to me in a little parcel last week, with a flag. What am I gonna do with a fucking flag? He picked up a teddy bear along the roadside, that's what his mates told me. I got an official call with all the bravery and valor shit attached—but it's because he picked up this little toy that a kid was pointing at. Blew David across the fucking street. Killed three others, including the little fella who told him to grab it in the first place. You believe that? Some bastard had a child of about eight do that. That's who they are—the same ones we share our city with and let come over here and do what they want . . . beat and rape and kill their women and shove 'em into suitcases when it's over, bury them in the back garden if they happen to fall in love with a boy they don't approve of . . . We put 'em through medical school while they sit in their flats and try to figure out new kinds of explosives to use on our buses and our tube . . . *That's* who killed the man I was going to marry next year . . . and they've won, by the way. They've already won, because we are completely terrified of them. It's like we used to feel about the blacks. Terrified. And why? Because the Muslims do what they say. They-follow-through. They are just crazy and off their heads enough to think that God is on their side and, well, if that's the case, anything goes! Hate the West and outsiders and other religions, and anything you feel like hating . . . that's fine. Just say Allah told me so and you're good to go. Do it in the name of Islam and who's gonna stop ya? Not Blair. That fucking child. And not Brown neither. (*Sets beret down.*) People used to say things about Bush all the time . . . say he's mad and all that, but I'll tell you one thing—he had his eyes on the prize and he never took 'em off it. And I, for one, think he was a whole lot sharper than people gave him credit for. At least he spoke his mind—not like this new one. *He* sounds like a fucking *preacher*. Bush may've had his own issues, but he never backed down if he wanted to say the Iraqis were evil and dirty and a small-minded people who were ungrateful for what we'd done for 'em. And I'll tell you one thing—Bush *never* would've picked up that bear. He'd've given that kid the finger and told him to pick up his own fucking bear. We think we're so much smarter here; telling it like it is. *The Guardian*? *The Independent*? I say bullshit. The newspapers are too afraid to say anything—to question, to judge, to expose these people. This is meant to be a free country where a person can speak their mind if they want to without getting the shit kicked out of them for it. Why does your average Muslim think we're afraid of 'em? Maybe because they stab filmmakers out in the street, or someone prints a cartoon in the paper and they receive death threats. *Death*. Somebody wants to kill 'em because of a picture they drew. Or a book they've written. I don't give a damn if you don't like Salman Rushdie but do you have to wanna *kill* 'em? They'll burn down embassies and butcher fucking nuns. You tell me where our fears come from? And now there's this new one. Right? This lady with her, something Jones, don't know her name, an American woman. She's done some book about Mohammed and his wife—first wife of however many—and it's supposed to be a bit trashy, a bit porno. But it's hers to write, isn't it? It's just fiction, some historical fiction with a bit of fucking in it and they're going crazy again. Twenty years after the last one and now they're firebombing the publisher. Lives in England, I read, lives here but he's Dutch. Ha! It's always the Dutch, isn't it? They're the only ones brave enough to stand up to these bastards—but yeah, his place was burned down and the book's on hold now. Nobody else will even pretend that they're going to publish it. And why? *Because* she has the *audacity* to say that this fellow, this man of God, actually made love to his wives. Wow! You know what I think? What they're *really* afraid of? If this keeps up, some kind of detailed scrutiny of their lives, we in the West are going to figure out the real truth—that Muslim men, if left to their own devices, are all a bunch of fucking gays. Why else would they keep their women covered up all the time? So they can pretend they are fucking something other than what they are. Young boys, probably. Every last one of 'em actually prefers cock, but they can't bring themselves to face it. That's why they're so touchy about it, screaming out in public and killing people to keep them from guessing the truth. Muslims secretly savor cock and none more so than Mohammed himself. And if I want to say that, if I want to stand out on the green and say "Mohammed was a cocksucker!"—and I don't mean in the usual disparaging way, but I'm suggesting that, yes, he may be a prophet of God, but when nobody was looking he loved to get down on his knees and suck a nice big white Western cock—then I should be able to without fear of a bomb going off in fucking Marks and Spencer's. I'm just saying, and this is a gross generalization, but this is what's left of my boyfriend and I'm in a bit of a bad mood—so I'm saying that basically, yes, Muslims are a vicious, backward-thinking people who deserve all of the fear and wrath and hatred that we heap on their greasy little heads. And I, for one, am no longer going to be afraid to speak my mind if I'm sitting on a bus, or in the cinema or, or . . . if I'm sitting on the bus or in . . .

She stops for a moment, noticing a young man in the crowd. Silence. She stares at him. Finally, she speaks again.

YOUNG WOMAN   Sorry . . . sorry. I've lost . . . sorry. (*She starts to get up but sits back down.*) "If I'm sitting on a bus or in . . . " No. Sorry. I can't keep doing the piece right now. I've tried, but . . . it's . . . this is weird. Sorry. Sorry. Oh, fuck. (*To man in crowd.*) Piece of advice—if you're gonna spy on someone don't sit in the fucking *front*, okay? It might help. (*Out to audience.*) Could I get an usher in here please? Is there an usher . . . So is this gonna be the new thing you do, or what? Because . . . Sorry, but this is, I don't know, maybe the . . . I don't even know how many times this guy has shown up when I'm trying to perform and it's a bit . . . creepy. The thing is, the very scary thing is, I haven't told him about this, it's not in the paper or been scheduled in the regular . . . It's not just because he reads *Time Out!* This guy is everywhere I go and it's . . . Would someone come and help me? Great. So, you're just gonna sit there and pretend it's not you? Okay . . . so, we'll all just—why are you here? This has got to stop. Seriously . . . you have to stop this. It's freaky and it scares me . . . I'm not joking, it does . . . And he's not even . . . he won't even say anything to me now, won't explain himself or argue with me . . . We met at a reading. It was a new play and he was there—he introduced himself as a friend of the writer, which, shit, was probably not even true, but I never checked . . . Who checks on stuff like that? We had a drink, at the pub, seems fine, tells me about *his* play—surprise!—there's a part in it for me, he thinks I would be sooo fantastic, and could we maybe meet up to discuss it at some point—dinner, or whatever—"You have an e-mail?" I'm an actress and I flatter easily and that's my problem. I was an only child, we moved around a lot, I get off on people watching me—I don't know, but it was a mistake! And I have told him that—maybe a dozen times now. I'm sorry but I do not want to see you anymore and I don't want you doing this—showing up in the audience and sitting there looking at me. You're wearing a fucking *raincoat!* I mean, you're a walking cliché and I have had to put up with this for almost *two* years . . . I've stopped taking jobs, knowing that I will freeze if I see him again. The only place I can work is in the Olivier! Or go on tour—no, not even that, no, I take that back. I take that back because somebody has even shown up where? Do you want to tell them or shall I? Let's see? Edinburgh? And Bath? I was in a production of the Scottish play down there and . . . hey . . . you know what? Fuck it . . . I was in *Macbeth! Mac-beth!* Maybe

Neil LaBute

the curse will work and you'll get hit by a fucking *taxi* tonight! You idiot! You're a fucking . . . This is so . . . (*Stares him down and then back to crowd.*) Our names aren't published in any of the literature . . . I checked before I took the job, just to be sure . . . So I don't know what sort of fucking *sonar* you have that tells you where I'm gonna be at any one time, but let me try and make this clear, once more, in front of this group of very nice people: GET OFF MY TITS YOU UGLY LITTLE PIECE OF SHIT YOU MAKE ME SICK! And . . . nothing. So that's great. Look, I'm sorry that your mother didn't love you, or loved you too much, or somebody touched your willy at school. I am truly sorry for anything that happened in your childhood, but it's not my fault. Don't blame me. I really would've read your script, too, but it's . . . it's just too late now and I really think that you should go. I don't want to have to call the police but I will. I'm not afraid to stand up for myself. I did call once, about a year ago—I'm a singer as well, I don't know if any of you know that. Maybe not. Well . . . somebody knows. Don't they? Yeah. (*She looks at him.*) I took a job doing Gilbert and Sullivan on the Isle of Man . . . that's how bad it's got. Very strange place but a gorgeous little theater . . . and two weeks into the run this prick shows up. And shows up. And keeps showing up, performance after performance after performance. Never at the stage door. Doesn't ask me out for a drink anymore . . . he just appears. Sitting there. Close, so I can see him, then at the interval he's gone. You want to talk about terror? The *Taliban* could learn a thing or two from a cock like you. It got so bad that I would be crying before going out onstage. Management thought I was drinking or doing drugs or whatever. It was a "mutual" decision for me to leave the company—meaning they allowed me to clean out my dressing room. I went back to my hotel and thought, "You know what? Fuck this. I have rights." That's when I called the police. But he was gone. No record of him being there and he even . . . I don't know if you got out by boat, or . . . or . . . you swam . . . or how you did it

. . . but they couldn't find a ferry reservation, or a plane ticket, nothing. They looked at me like I was a total psycho thanks to you. It was completely fucked that you did that to me. Once, this one time—it wasn't even at a show! He didn't even give me the courtesy of getting cast before he starts doing his thing. I'm at an audition for the Peter Hall Company, a really big deal for an out-of-town show, Chichester Festival (a Chekhov play with Dame Judi Dench), so yes, I was a little bit excited—and Mr. McPervert here is in the hallway, down on the floor, curled up with a book and watching me. Doesn't say a word. Remember? This is the first time he starts doing this shit. No more talking. Now he just watches me. I'm so angry and put off that I go up to tell the girl what's going on and I turn around so I can point him out and of course . . . he's gone. *Poof.* Vanished. And I'm standing there like some crazy fucking actress girl, so finally I just gather up my stuff, I toss everything back into my bag, and I go. I blow it off. *Peter* Hall, because of Norman fucking Bates here who keeps showing up at my places of work! If you could see all of the locks I've added onto the door of my flat and the windows . . . you would laugh in my face. Seriously. I think you would. My housemates do. Yes. I have *housemates* again, at my age. Two students, because I am scared to death of living alone now. Thanks to you. You, you motherfucker. *You.* This is what I deal with . . . (*Beat.*) And now here. To show up here . . . People just want a bit of entertainment for their money . . . and you've now ruined it, an original monologue written for me, for *me*, by a real writer . . . but you've just got to have your . . . Excuse me, where are the fucking ushers here? You know what, fuck it, I'll do it myself. That's it. I'm drawing a fucking line in the sand, right now.

She physically makes the move with her shoe—as if pulling her toe slowly through the sand.

YOUNG WOMAN   I will not move. I'm gonna stand right here, and you know what? These people will all think it's part of the performance . . . but we *know*. Right? You and me? We know what's what. And I'm not letting you out of my sight. See how you like it. Prick. Cock. See how much *you* like being followed and stared at. You cunt. Go on. Make a run for it. Do it. Go on. Do it! I fucking dare you. The door is just round there. You can make it. I know you can. You're a guy. You're much faster than I am. *Maybe.* That's what you're trying to decide, isn't it? Can I get to my feet and run? You could probably make it to the tube without me catching you if you didn't have that fucking *raincoat* on . . . There's a chance anyway. But if not . . . on the off chance that I keep up with you and jump on your same train . . . you're fucked. You can walk around all night, or go to the police or a friend's place, whatever . . . but eventually I'm gonna find out where you live. So . . . (*She goes and closes the "exit" door. Quietly locks it.*) Did you ever see any of those movies from the seventies where a woman—or a lady and her friend—get the shit kicked out of them, or raped, for about half the film, and then finally, just when it's almost too much to take, they fight back? They buy a gun, or they escape their shackles, and they go on this completely mental rampage . . . to avenge what has happened to them. Stabbing these guys with pitchforks, or blowing their bollocks off. That is gonna be me today. I am gonna follow you, and hunt you down and then I will bury you. I shit you not. This is the last time you'll *ever* do this to anyone. It's over. As of today. (*She stops, checking on his reaction. She steps closer.*) You're scared aren't you? You are. Afraid to let these people see who you are, and scared to death of showing your true self to me or anybody else . . . (*Smiles.*) Well, guess what? I don't care. This is me putting an end to your little reign of terror. So I dare you. I do. I fucking dare you to do it. Come on. Right now. Come on, you fucker! This is it! This is the moment where I take my life back. I'm taking it back right now, you dirty piece of shit! I am declaring *war* on you, so come on!

Make your move. Do it! Do it. DO IT NOW, YOU PUSSY! You're a fucking pussy and you make me sick! (*Waits for him to move. Takes a few steps closer to him.*) Come the fuck on. Are you ready? I said, "Are you ready, motherfucker?!" You better be, because this is it! Do you hear me?! This is it! THIS IS FUCKING IT!

She suddenly bolts forward, toward the young man. The lights go out just before she reaches him. Music up. Unbearably loud.

Silence. Darkness.

helter
skelter

production history

Helter Skelter had its world premiere in March 2007 at the Theatre Bonn in Bonn, Germany, in a production directed by Jennifer Whigham.

This play has also been performed in the United States under the title *Things We Said Today* (most notably in its New York City debut in June 2007, in a production directed by Andrew McCarthy).

characters

MAN   in his late thirties
WOMAN   in her mid-thirties

setting

A chic little eatery.

time

Right around the holidays.

NOTE: While *Helter Skelter* is a theatrical entertainment, it is meant to be played as honestly as possible so that the ending remains truly surprising. The "blood" effect at the end is of particular importance and should be bluntly real (red streamers or something equally artsy is not enough). If suggestions are needed on how to execute this moment properly, please contact the author via the Gersh agency in New York City.

Silence. Darkness.

A MAN *sitting at a table in some chic restaurant, sipping a drink. After a bit, he checks his watch. Muzak playing.*

A WOMAN *arrives, carrying a shitload of packages. The* MAN *stands and helps her with the stack—we see now that she is pregnant. Very.*

A kiss happens. Nothing amazing, just a peck. She sits.

WOMAN   . . . 's crazy out there.

MAN   I know.

WOMAN   I mean, seriously. It's, like, *seriously* crazy on the street today.

MAN   I agree.

WOMAN   People shopping.

MAN   Right.

WOMAN   They'll kill you. They would actually be happy to *kill* you if it'll help them . . .

MAN   I'm sure.

WOMAN   With a spot in line or something. To grab the last . . . whatever-it-is that they want.

MAN   Or *think* they want . . .

WOMAN   Exactly! It's amazing.

MAN   Uh-huh.

WOMAN   And a little frightening. Christmas.

MAN   Every year . . .

WOMAN   God! It's . . . (*Beat.*) I love it.

They look at each other and burst out laughing. Ho-ho-ho.

MAN   I picked up a few items—that video game they want. (*Beat.*) And you? Anything good?

WOMAN   Oh, you know, a couple things . . . little stuff, for the kids. My sister. Nothing that's gonna matter two months from now, but it's a start. (*Beat.*) Imagine if we'd waited until after the holiday—if we'd come down here the weekend *after* Thanksgiving? It'd be, well . . . absolute chaos.

MAN Oh, yeah.

WOMAN You know? Unreal . . . Already it's, like, so unpleasant, so out of the realm of how it should be, the delicious fun that you can remember from your childhood . . .

MAN Whole thing's been commercialized.

WOMAN That's right.

MAN Turned into an advertising circus . . .

WOMAN Yes. It's . . .

MAN . . . a shame, really . . .

WOMAN It absolutely is—and a *sham!* It's both.

MAN . . . oh, well. (*Laughs.*) What're ya gonna do?

WOMAN I don't know. Complain?

MAN I suppose . . .

WOMAN That's about it. Max out those cards and complain to someone you love . . .

MAN So true.

WOMAN Cozy up with a loved one in a chic little eatery and bitch about the state of things. It's the way of the world . . .

MAN I agree. And we can do just that—either here or once we get back to the hotel . . .

WOMAN Perfect. (*Beat.*) 'S what we do every year, isn't it?

MAN Mmm-hmmm.

WOMAN How many times have we done this? I mean, these little shopping getaways?

MAN Ohhhh, God . . . at least since we moved. If not that first Christmas than at least by the . . . yes, second one for sure.

WOMAN That's what I was thinking. At least that long.

MAN Yep. (*Beat.*) They're fun, right?

MAN *takes a gulp of his drink, finishes it. Holds up his hand. He glances at the* WOMAN *and smiles. She returns it.*

MAN You want anything? I could easily do with another one . . .

WOMAN Sure. Yes. Bloody Mary, maybe? (*Grins.*) I'm kidding . . .

MAN 'Course. (*Grins back.*) So?

WOMAN . . . surprise me.

He stands up to go off and get the order filled. She puts up a hand, stopping him.

WOMAN Do you have your phone?

MAN Hmm?

WOMAN Your cell . . . do you have it on you?

MAN I'm . . . sure, yes. It's right . . .

He starts to feel his jacket, patting the pockets as he searches. She watches him while removing her own phone from a purse.

WOMAN I ran mine out of battery. (*Smiles.*) You can take *satellite* photos with it but it can't hold a charge for more than, like, *two* minutes!

MAN . . . that's so true . . .

WOMAN Did you find it?

MAN Yeah, it's . . . one of these pockets . . .

WOMAN I just want to call the sitter. See how the kids're doing . . .

MAN Lemme see . . . it's . . . I called them earlier, by the way, said "hi." They were fine.

WOMAN . . . good. (*Waits.*) You don't have it?

MAN Maybe I . . . Did I leave it in the room?

WOMAN No . . .

MAN I didn't?

WOMAN Uh-uh. Impossible . . . I called you before lunch, remember? *And* you rang the kids.

MAN Oh, right . . . so . . .

WOMAN Did you try the inside one? I've seen you put it in there before . . .

MAN *reaches inside his jacket. Feels around. Nothing.*

MAN   Nope.

WOMAN   Huh.

MAN   Can you believe that? Maybe I've . . . Did I leave it somewhere? In the sporting goods store, or that . . . ? God, I hate this!

WOMAN   It's not in that pocket, right there?

MAN   Hmmm?

WOMAN   There . . . where the bulge is. That one.

MAN   No, it's . . . I checked that one already.

WOMAN   You did?

MAN   Yes, when I first . . .

WOMAN   Just try it again. Please. (*Beat.*) For me.

MAN   Fine, but I . . . (*Feels inside.*) Nothing.

WOMAN   Really?

MAN   No . . . (*He pulls out his wallet.*) See?

WOMAN   Oh, it's your . . . sorry, I thought that shape was your . . .

The MAN *is close enough to her—she suddenly reaches over and feels the pocket for herself.*

MAN   What're you doing? Hold on!

WOMAN   There . . . isn't that it? Right there?

MAN   That's . . .

WOMAN   I can feel it. In the corner.

The MAN *reaches in and digs around—makes it look a bit elaborate. He finally retrieves it.*

MAN   Ah, there it is! Got stuck in the fabric.

WOMAN   Was that it?

MAN   Yes. Tucked up in that, you know . . . bit of cloth where the pocket attaches to the . . .

WOMAN   I see. (*Puts her hand out.*) May I?

MAN   Ummm, yeah, lemme just . . . I'm . . .

WOMAN   I can dial it.

MAN   Fine, go ahead, I just wanna . . .

WOMAN I'll do it.

MAN Wait, I'd like to make sure . . .

She gets a hand on the thing as the MAN *is pulling away—the phone crashes to the ground. Shatters.*

WOMAN . . . oh.

MAN Now look what you've done! God . . . (*Picks up the pieces.*) I don't think I can even get this to . . . Why did you have to . . . ?

He struggles with the battery, trying to replace it. She watches him carefully.

WOMAN Do you want me to . . . ?

MAN I've got it. *Wait.* (*Fighting it*) Damn!

WOMAN What?

MAN I think the case is . . . I can hear a piece of it rattling around in there. Listen.

He shakes the thing and it does indeed rattle. She frowns at this.

WOMAN Well, it's . . . or maybe you can . . .

MAN Maybe it's broken, okay? *Maybe* that's the story . . . my phone got broke.

WOMAN Sorry.

MAN It's . . . doesn't matter.

WOMAN I *am* sorry. (*Beat.*) Do they have a . . . ?

MAN No, I'm not gonna go wandering around the city, looking for a place where they can fix the thing, I'm not doing that . . .

WOMAN . . . I wasn't suggesting that . . . you . . .

MAN Let's just get our stuff together and go back to the hotel. You can call from in there . . .

WOMAN Fine. (*Beat.*) Are you sure you didn't just turn the battery over by mistake? I know that in the past I've . . .

MAN Will you *stop*? Please? I'm sorry but I do not want this becoming some . . . big . . . *thing* here, okay? One of those Greek dramas . . .

WOMAN It won't, I'm just trying to . . . although I don't know what you've got against a "big thing" happening . . . if it's worth it.

MAN We'll be back in fifteen minutes. Can the kids wait for a few seconds or do ya have to get on a line *this* instant? Huh?

WOMAN . . . I can wait.

MAN Good.

WOMAN Yes.

MAN Thank you.

WOMAN I'll be happy to wait until we get back. (*Beat.*) If . . .

MAN What?

WOMAN I said: if. *If* you do something for me . . .

MAN Now what? God! I mean, look, I'm . . .

Before answering, the WOMAN *stands up. Holds out her arms.*

WOMAN Would you help me with this coat? Seems very hot in here suddenly . . .

MAN Of course.

He hops back to his feet and moves to the WOMAN—*leaves the phone on the table.*

She removes each arm from the jacket and then stands to smooth out her dress—it is long and icy white. She is wearing pearls with it.

As he goes to sit she snatches the cell from the table and pops it into her handbag.

MAN Don't do that . . . What're you doing?!

WOMAN What I said I'd do—but without your help.

MAN Honey . . .

WOMAN I promised myself, just now, that if you handed it over—your cell—without some . . . *elaborate* game, then fine. I'd let it go at that . . . but you didn't. You did not, so . . . I'm resorting to this.

MAN What're you . . . I don't get what you're . . . ?

WOMAN I'm going to wait and fix it, when we get back—I'll put it all back together and plug it in and then I'll turn it on. Do you hear me? I will turn on your phone and watch it light up and then I'll check the last few numbers you dialed. Today. (*Beat.*) That's what I'm going to do . . .

The MAN *stares at her. Speechless. He slowly sits down in his chair.*

MAN You're . . . What're you *doing*? Sweetie?

WOMAN I just told you.

MAN No, I *know*, but I mean . . . why're you being all . . . so . . . (*Beat.*) And why're you wearing that *dress*? It seems a little . . . something for shopping . . .

WOMAN It probably is. (*Beat.*) A little what?

MAN Ummm . . . "summery," maybe? Or . . . I dunno. Youthful?

WOMAN Hmmm. Well . . . (*Beat.*) It felt right this morning, when we were getting ready.

MAN Oh.

WOMAN You didn't notice it then . . . when you were getting on your slacks and your shirt, it didn't seem "a little something" then?

MAN I guess I . . . I didn't realize. No.

WOMAN You were going in and out of the room . . .

MAN Yes, I know . . .

WOMAN . . . back and forth into the other part of the suite, doing things. *Texting*. (*Beat.*) It never struck you as too much then?

MAN I didn't . . . sorry, no. Just now is all.

WOMAN I see. (*Studies him.*) You can sit again if you'd like . . .

MAN I'm not sure yet.

WOMAN Really?

MAN No, I . . . I dunno. You're acting . . . all . . .

The MAN *looks around, realizes that this is pretty silly, then sits back down. Checks his watch.*

MAN Listen . . . honey . . . we can . . . I can probably get the thing to work, if you just give me a minute with it. I'm . . .

WOMAN I know you can. Of course you can.

MAN So, then, lemme . . . you know. Let me do it back at the hotel, when we're alone . . .

WOMAN No, I'd rather do it myself, actually.

MAN Come on, let's not . . .

WOMAN That's what I want to do. Okay?

MAN No, it's not, *actually!* It's not okay. I'm actually kind of sick of this behavior . . . (*Beat.*) I mean, what're you doing with all this, huh? Some kind of . . . I dunno . . .

WOMAN Who do you think it's going to be?

MAN What? (*Waits.*) Excuse me?

WOMAN The first number I find there—which'll be the last one, really, right? The one that comes up first'll be the one that you called most recently . . .

MAN . . . yes, but . . .

WOMAN I'm curious . . . who?

MAN It's . . . ummmm, lemme think.

WOMAN Any idea?

MAN Probably . . . no, not you . . . I was . . .

WOMAN Got it?

MAN No, but . . . oh, I know who it's gonna be—and this should be nice and embarrassing for you—it's your sister! That's who.

WOMAN Really?

MAN Yes.

WOMAN And why's that?

MAN Because . . . sweetie, look around you. Okay? It's the holidays. You're not exactly the easiest person to shop for . . .

WOMAN Ahhh.

MAN Yeah, "ahhh." (*Beat.*) I called her to get some gift ideas and, and . . . you know, we talked for a bit, I asked her how things were going at school, that sort of deal. Had a nice little chat.

WOMAN I'll bet.

MAN Now what's that supposed to mean?

WOMAN Just that. I'll bet you had a nice chat.

Neil LaBute

MAN We did.

WOMAN I'll bet . . .

MAN Look, I'm . . .

WOMAN I'll just bet you did.

MAN All right, this is getting kind of . . .

WOMAN What? Tell me.

MAN I don't know! Silly, I guess.

WOMAN You think I'm being *silly* now? Is that what you think? That I'm . . .

MAN Yes, I do. A bit.

WOMAN I'm sorry . . .

MAN It's fine, it's probably just the . . . you know, being pregnant and the walking all over the . . . shopping, right?

WOMAN Yes, that's true. I walked all over.

MAN Really?

WOMAN Uh-huh—further than I thought I would. Further than I told you I would.

MAN You did?

WOMAN Much. Much, *much* further. (*She starts to tear up.*) Oh yes . . .

He starts to move, to stand and go to her but she stops him with a word.

WOMAN Stay! Sit down and stay right there . . . no. (*He reaches out.*) Don't.

MAN But I'm . . . honey, you're . . .

WOMAN How long?

MAN What?

WOMAN I'm asking "how long?" If I hadn't walked past her street, down past the park and all the way over by the water—I was thinking about that little cheese shop at the end of her block, the one that you've always *loved*—if I hadn't done that and seen you, watched the two of you out there on her steps . . . the steps *out*side, that lead up into her house, how long would you say that this has been going on? Hmmm?

MAN I'm . . . it's . . . (*Beat.*) I can't really . . .

WOMAN Yes, you can! You can find within you the very last decent thing that might happen in these circumstances and you can say to me how long this has been happening.

MAN . . . no.

WOMAN Yes, you can.

MAN But . . . we're . . . Jesus . . .

WOMAN It'll hurt less if you just do it—like when they shoot an animal. Quickly helps. (*Beat.*) Go on. *Please.*

MAN Fine—six years.

WOMAN . . . years?

MAN Yes.

WOMAN *Years*? Did I hear you correctly? Did you say *"years"*?

MAN I did, yes. Six.

WOMAN So . . . since before her divorce? And . . .

MAN Uh-huh.

WOMAN Before she left her husband . . . *before* that time, you two were . . . on her steps there? So to speak . . .

MAN I s'pose. (*Beat.*) It's been a while now . . .

WOMAN I see.

MAN Right before we moved to the new house. Off to the suburbs, I mean . . .

WOMAN Really?

MAN Around there. I didn't write it down or anything, so I'm . . . it's a guess.

WOMAN Got it.

MAN I'm not proud of this.

WOMAN Well, that's something.

MAN I'm not . . . listen, I want you to hear me on this, one thing about this before . . .

WOMAN Yes?

MAN I dunno, before you go and get all . . . you know, worked up about it. Or however you do. (*Thinks.*) This is only one little part of me, the man that I am. *Me.* I'm an okay guy, basically, and I think you know that fact. You do. I've always been—this all sounds ridiculous now, but . . . I'm a person who loves you, and the kids, too, which I know that you rationally believe to be a truth as well. It is, it's true. (*Beat.*) I didn't want this

to happen but it started out as a comforting thing and it just
. . . well, it just grew. The way things do. It took on a life of its
own and I can't say it's wrong or immoral or whatnot because
that would be hurtful to the little good that has come from
it—and some has, if you believe it or not—there have been
times when a few moments of . . . you know . . . kept me
feeling sane. Or normal. Something. So it's not my place to
badmouth it so that I can try and save face here, with you.
That's what a *lesser* man would do. (*Beat.*) I'm sure you feel
differently and that's okay, that's expected, but I just want
to say that we're not all one thing, right? Good or bad or like
that. We're just . . . people, folks who make mistakes, who
do good or bad *things* but they aren't really what defines us.
(*Beat.*) I see you glaring at me and that look in your eyes and
I'm not defending myself, I'm not, I'm really just saying, "Hey,
honey, it's still me. I'm still the guy you married." I'm very
sorry to have hurt you and I don't feel proud of—no, I'm just
gonna leave it at that. I'm sorry.

The WOMAN *has listened to all of this quietly. Taking it in. She waits
yet another beat.*

WOMAN   . . . and is she? Do you have any idea?

MAN   What?

WOMAN   Is she's proud of what's happened? My *sister.*

MAN   No, I don't—I mean, we don't really talk about it much,
so . . .

WOMAN   No?

MAN   Well . . . yes, obviously we *speak*, I'm not saying that, but
. . . it's mostly, you know. What you saw. There. (*Beat.*) It's
physical.

WOMAN   Right.

MAN   Anyway . . .

WOMAN   Is it at all hard saying something like that, or do you find
that it just spills out of your mouth . . . ? Hmm?

MAN   Look . . . I'm trying to be adult about this.

WOMAN   Why? (*Beat.*) Why now?

MAN Honey . . .

WOMAN I don't get that part. When people have done the most outrageous . . . shit, right? When you go and do this completely bad and adolescent thing that will hurt *so* many people and is just, like, off the charts, out-of-this-world insane—sure to cause the downfall of an entire . . . *family* for years to come, how come the urge immediately afterwards is to always get sensible? Huh?

MAN I don't know.

WOMAN *Why?*

MAN I'm . . . maybe because it's . . .

WOMAN Why would that be? (*Beat.*) How come it's never *before*—just before you lean over and kiss the woman who is married to a friend of yours and is related by blood to the woman you're sleeping with . . . the lady that you've filled up with the *seed* of your loins . . . (*Pointing at her belly.*) Do you even see this? What's going on, right *here*?

MAN Of course I do . . .

WOMAN Well, that's good. That's the best news I've had all day . . . (*Smiles.*) And you two never thought about just saying something to me, or, like, running off to some . . . you know, *tropical* isle or like that?

MAN No.

WOMAN Why not? Why not go for broke with this, since it's already taken on all these . . . *biblical* proportions. Hmmm?

MAN I'm not sure . . . (*Beat.*) I did want to, if you must know. A few years ago.

WOMAN Really?

MAN Yes. I even . . . I dunno, drew up the plans for it all—the itineraries or whatever.

WOMAN Ahhh. (*Remembering now.*) *Maps?*

MAN Excuse me?

WOMAN You know . . . the little guidebooks, with the maps tucked inside. (*Beat.*) I seem to remember some of those showing up around the house. "A few years ago." Was that a coincidence, or . . . ?

MAN . . . yes. I mean, no. (*Beat.*) I bought them.

WOMAN Perfect.

MAN But she didn't want to . . . your sister did not want to go through with it, so I put the tickets back on the charge card and I didn't worry about it again . . .

WOMAN "Tickets." *Wow.* (*Dazed.*) And why not?

MAN What do you mean?

WOMAN My sis-ter. Why didn't she want to leave with you to points unknown? Whyever not?

MAN I think she . . . no, I *know* this, actually. For a fact. She didn't want to hurt you.

The WOMAN *turns and looks at him—they remain in silence for a moment. Suddenly, she bursts out laughing. Really laughing. Hysterics.*

The MAN *watches for a moment, then looks around. Finally he tries to calm her.*

MAN . . . honey. Stop. Come on, stop it. Will you please . . . sweetie, stop this. Stop. Stop it! *Stop!*

And as suddenly as she began, the WOMAN *does stop. It is deathly quiet again.*

MAN You're making a scene . . .

A last little burst slips out of her mouth—she throws a hand over her lips and stops. Wild-eyed.

WOMAN I'm sorry—don't know what came over me.

MAN It's okay, I understand, but . . . you know.

WOMAN No, what? What should I know?

MAN We're . . . this is in *public.* So . . .

WOMAN I see. (*Beat.*) Like when I saw you with my sister out there on her porch? Like that kind of "in public"?

MAN . . . I guess. Yes.

WOMAN I see. Just wanted to be clear.

MAN Fine.

WOMAN Make sure we're talking the same language here and all that . . .

MAN 'Kay.

WOMAN . . . because I certainly wouldn't want to cause a misunderstanding between us. To be the one who creates a *rift* in our . . . little lives. God forbid I do that!

MAN Honey, can we just, please . . . ?

WOMAN What?

MAN I dunno. I was just throwing it out there to, you know . . . maybe get things started. To *jump*start this. Get us out of here . . .

WOMAN Oh. I see. (*Beat.*) Then, no . . .

MAN "No" what? (*Beat.*) All right, this is going nowhere, so . . . look, I think I should . . .

He clears his throat and leans in closer to his wife. He speaks a bit more quietly now.

MAN Let's clear the air here, all right? I do not want you to . . . to take this on your shoulders, to carry the burden of this. I don't. (*Tries to smile.*) It's a mess, I'm aware of that, I know it, but it's not what I . . . what I'd wanted for us. *Any* of us. This is one of those things . . . You know when you hear someone say, "It just happened," well, that's exactly the case here! Yes, it happened and it's wrong and all that, I realize that part of it, I do. But what're you gonna *do*, right? I mean, we've very logically and naturally come to this juncture and the more we . . . I don't know what I'm trying to say, but the harder that we work to place blame on somebody's back, the worse off we're all going to be in the end . . . I can feel it. (*Beat.*) We can be civil about this, seems to me, civil and, and understanding and work toward clarity . . . work together for a better tomorrow. I'm just babbling on here, but I think there's some truth in what I'm saying—tomorrow is another day and you and I are going to learn from all this, to grow and become richer, better people because of it, we really are, and I'm including your sister here . . . adding her into the mix because, believe me, I've spoken about all this with her—at least over the course of these six years that we've—it doesn't matter. No, what's important right now is healing. A sense of love and forgiveness that the children can feel, no matter how much we tell them about this . . . and I vote for very little here, actually; I think complete knowledge now would do nothing but breed heartache and resentment and, and, like, *fury* for no good reason. (*Beat.*) Honey—bear with me on this, okay, because I'm just thinking out loud here, but I feel pretty—listen, we can get through this. We can. I don't know how exactly or in what configuration yet, but we'll get through it. Through it and, and you know what? Maybe even on to some better thing. That probably sounds . . . but maybe so. We might. We could still break through to some richer and more . . . *beautiful* place because of what we've done here . . . your sister and me. (*Beat.*) So, ummm . . . can we go now? Honey?

WOMAN No, no . . . this is perfect. Right here. In this restaurant.

He looks around. It seems perfectly ordinary to him.

MAN I don't get why . . . Are you hungry?

WOMAN No, I'm not . . . no. I just don't want to be alone with you. I don't want that, ever again—after that . . . what you just *spewed*—so I'm very happy to stay right here . . .

MAN Well, yeah, but . . . I mean, you can't stay here the rest of your life. Right? Okay, yes, we have some things to work out . . . to talk about, but . . . we can't . . .

WOMAN How do you know that? Hmmm?

MAN I don't know what you're . . . I'm lost.

WOMAN Why can't I be here for the rest of my life? How can you be so sure this isn't the last place I'll ever visit?

MAN Because that's . . . it's *not*, so . . . you know.

WOMAN No, I don't. I've realized today that I do not know anything—*every*thing that I thought I knew or believed has flown out the window and I'm starting from scratch. I mean, yes, normally I would meet you in here and have a drink or dinner and we'd leave at the end, life goes on . . . but now, after what has happened to me . . . how do I know this isn't the last place on earth for me? Or you? How would I really *know*?

MAN   This is . . . listen, let me get you back to the room and I'll . . . I'll go home, head up on the train so you can . . . please . . .

WOMAN   Because you don't want to create a scene, right? That's it, isn't it?

MAN   . . . no, I just . . .

WOMAN   Tell me the truth. For *once*—apparently—just say what's true. (*Beat.*) That's what it is for most people, so . . .

MAN   No . . . I mean, yes, that's true, the idea of us having some knockdown, drag-out in the middle of this place isn't my idea of a great day, *obviously*, but no . . . this is me thinking about you now. And the baby.

WOMAN   Ohhhh, right. Yes. Of course. The baby. *Our* baby. That I'm carrying . . .

MAN   Yes.

WOMAN   Which, if I'm not mistaken, I had inside me a few hours ago, back when I was down the street from you and watching you put your tongue into my sister's mouth, your hands going up and down her body, across her soft skin—you mean that baby, right? The one right . . . (*Points.*) . . . *here*.

MAN   That one. Yes, I do mean that one. (*Beat.*) So, can we go? Honey?

WOMAN   No, I told you already . . . I don't want to be alone with you ever again. That rules out the hotel, even with you leaving for home . . . because I can't fathom standing up and you helping me with my coat and us walking out together—you carrying these packages because you think that somehow that'll *mean* something—and helping get me back to the hotel, upstairs with all the other guests in the elevator, having to feel you pressed up against me since it's crowded and one of those smiles that you do when we've . . . *no.* That can't be.

They sit for a moment, waiting for something else to be said—for now there is only silence.

MAN   . . . I could put you in a cab. What about that? I'll just run
   out and . . .
WOMAN   No. (*Beat.*) You're thinking logically now and you need to
   quit that . . .
MAN   *Honey* . . .
WOMAN   Stop saying that! "Honey." (*Beat.*) Now, you've got to
   stop being so practical . . .
MAN   . . . why don't you let me just . . .
WOMAN   No, I said. *No.* (*Beat.*) No . . . cabs or train fares or
   calling our lawyers after making it through the holiday for the
   kids' sake and all the rest of it. *No!*

She slams the tabletop with the palms of her hands for a bit of emphasis. The china rattles. The MAN *looks around.*

MAN   Well, what then? I mean, I'm trying to . . .
WOMAN   What? Finish that sentence, please.
MAN   . . . *hoping* to . . . forget it. I tried. (*Beat.*) Go ahead.

Another little burst of laughter; she can't control it.

WOMAN   Sorry.
MAN   It's not funny . . .
WOMAN   No, I agree with you. I so, *so* agree with you on that. It's
   not. At all. Funny.

Another burst overtakes her; she fights to overcome it.

WOMAN   Forgive me . . .
MAN   Whatever.
WOMAN   Yes. Whatever. Like the kids say . . . now I understand
   what they're getting at.
MAN   Hmm?

WOMAN What-*ever* . . . (*Beat.*) You know how I think this should end? Us?

MAN . . . how?

WOMAN Spectacularly. Vividly. *Operatically.*

MAN What does that mean? (*Changing tone.*) I'm, listen, I feel terrible about this, that you'd find out the way you did . . . Can't I just try and make it up to you? I know it might take a, a, a long . . . but can't I?

She stares at him for a moment in complete silence. An almost serene sense of peace seems to overtake her.

WOMAN Oh no. No, nothing like that. Don't think so plainly now . . . you've plotted and planned like a military general for years—*years*—at least help me finish it off with some of the glory and astonishment that this union of ours deserves . . . *please* do that.

MAN . . . but . . .

WOMAN We don't think outside the box anymore, do you realize that? Not just you and me, but everybody, that's what I'm saying . . . The world has come to a stop. We're off our rockers, completely mad, but we just keep limping along, acting like it's all okay and nothing out of the ordinary could be happening . . . happening right under our very noses! And all we want to do is get on with it, to, to keep going to work and down to the grocery store and off on vacation in the summer and that's it, that's enough for most of us. Each morning we pick up the paper over our cereal and we see . . .

She stops for a moment, marveling at this thought.

WOMAN . . . my God, the *things* that we're witness to! Tsunamis and hatred and atrocities of such magnitude that it takes your breath away . . . really, sucks it right out of your lungs and whisks it away; but you know what fools us, tricks us into thinking that it isn't really happening down the block and in our state and across the ocean? We get used to it always

Neil LaBute

being somebody else. It is *always* some other person who has their legs blown off in the marketplace . . . never you that gets into the auto accident that sends you smashing through the windshield and having to have your face rebuilt, no, it never is . . . Why is that? I don't know. (*Beat.*) So we go along believing that our children will grow up strong and true and that our husbands will be faithful and we plan on dying peacefully in our sleep and *that* is how we kid ourselves into taking the next step and the next one and each one after that . . . (*Turns to the* MAN.) But I don't believe that anymore. Those kinds of lies. I believe we're *extraordinary* . . . each one of us, capable of such amazing things and phenomenal heights. I really do. But do we do it? Do we go off and do those things—nail our demands up on the door of a church, making ourselves heard *each* and every day? *No*, is the answer . . . no, we don't. Not most of us. The things we say today are forgotten at the second, the very *second* that they slip from our mouths . . . (*Thinking.*) You'd like nothing more than for me to go quietly right now, leave this place and accept a quick divorce . . . and maybe no one at your work would even realize that some change had occurred in your life! I do believe that's what you wish could happen, there in your heart of hearts—and I'm giving you the benefit of the doubt on ownership of that particular organ—but that isn't what's going to happen here. It's not, my dear, no, it's not . . . so get that idea right out of your head.

She sits, waiting for an answer—the MAN *shrugs. Silent. She is about to say something but she catches herself. A tiny smile.*

WOMAN As children we do nothing but read all these stories . . . tales of wonder and of myth. *Legends.* And we never question if they're real or imagined—we just simply believe. Medea and Joan of Arc and, and the girls who followed Charles Manson up a hill one fateful night . . . they were all just people at one time . . . like you and me and anyone else. (*Beat.*) And then a thing happens, some *thing* happens inside them or *to* them, they wake up or get pushed off a ledge, a light turns off or on and *snap!* They are never the same again—and off they go on their merry way. Maybe to wander about the city first . . . block after block, trying to convince themselves that what they saw wasn't really true but they know it is, they *know* it, and that's when they stop and buy a dress, a dress that is perhaps too young for them, yes, far too "*youth*ful," but it reminds them of a time when they were lovely and carefree and of an age before they'd ever-even-heard-your-name—you were correct about what I wore out of the hotel this morning, good for you!—and then they make their way over to a restaurant where they know their husband will be waiting for them but *that's* how it happens to people. People just like me—real and normal and not at all fantastic or anything special; this is the *only* way that many of us will ever have the world turn its weary head toward us one time in our entire lives. This is how we become . . . *remembered.*

MAN What're you talking about? Honey . . . sorry, *sweetie* . . . I don't get what you're saying.

WOMAN You don't? Really?

MAN No . . . I mean, I follow you, some of your ideas there, but you're not making any . . . sense . . . you're . . .

WOMAN Here's what I'm saying—*this* is how it all begins. With a single step. (*Beat.*) *This* . . . is . . . what . . . we . . . become . . .

Without warning, the WOMAN *picks up a steak knife off the table and plunges it into her protruding belly. It sticks there, wedged deep inside her flesh. Her eyes grow wider but she remains lucid, even as she screams out.*

WOMAN *Aaaaaaaawwwwwwwwwwwwww!*

Somehow she pulls it out, then slams it back in. Deeper.

The MAN *is frozen for a moment. When he finally reacts, it is too late—he reaches for the* WOMAN *but she is too quick for him; she has scooped up his knife and holds it in her hands. Pointing it at him.*

MAN   Oh my God . . . oh my God . . . *oh my God!*
WOMAN   Now . . . what . . . do . . . you . . . do? Now . . . what?

The crimson stain is growing on her dress. The MAN *can't seem to decide what to do. He shuffles back and forth.*

MAN   *Oh my God . . . Somebody help . . . Help us!*
WOMAN   Now what?
MAN   *Help us, please! Somebody! Somebody help!*
WOMAN   Now . . .
MAN   *Help! Please help!! Please! Help me!!*

The WOMAN *continues to hold the knife, pointed toward the* MAN; *he finally bolts and runs off. Desperate. Exits.*

WOMAN   . . . what?

The WOMAN *slowly turns out toward us—carefully puts the knife down on the table. Sits back. Hands on her belly. The stain continues to spread.*

Sound of Muzak growing to a roar. Overtaking everything.

Silence. Darkness.